D0901690

# ONE HUNDRED WHISPERS

## AN ASPEN COVE SMALL TOWN ROMANCE

### KELLY COLLINS

BOOK NOOK PRESS

Copyright © 2021 by Kelley Maestas

No part of this publication may be reproduced, distributed, or transmitted in any form or by any means, including photocopying, recording, or other electronic or mechanical methods, without the prior written permission of the publisher, except as permitted by U.S. copyright law. For permission requests, contact kelly@ authorkellycollins.com.

The story, all names, characters, and incidents portrayed in this production are fictitious. No identification with actual persons (living or deceased), places, buildings, and products is intended or should be inferred. All products or brand names are trademarks of their respective owners.

# CHAPTER ONE

Jewel Monroe stood three rungs from the top of the ladder, unfastening the shelving put there decades ago.

"Didn't they have screws back then?" She looked around the store, making sure no one had snuck in while she turned her back to the door. Zoning out had become a thing lately. Focused on more significant issues like her mounting failures had made her feel like someone with a personality disorder. Who people said she was and who she really was, was different. Add in her impulsive decision to buy a run-down country store in a town with fewer people than the sets where she used to work, and she wondered if she'd gone crazy. Most days, her brain hurt too much to think, or maybe it was her heart.

If she didn't constantly make lists, she might get nothing done.

A giggle left her lips. Lately, her lists were more comical than practical. Yesterday she'd made one with fifty ways to kill her ex-husband. It started with quick and relatively painless electrocution. He was always screwing up the breaker boxes to the homes they restored so it would be a plausible accidental death. It ended with death by nail gun. Less believable but so much more satisfying to implement. When she finished her list and stopped fantasizing about his slow and painful demise, she tore it into tiny shreds. If Matthew Monroe ended up dead, having a list with fifty painful ways to do the deed wouldn't help her confirm her innocence if charged.

"I would've started crotch level and worked my way to his hollow heart," she said as she considered the nail gun once more.

She tugged at the shelf with its rusty nails, hoping it would give way and come tumbling down. The rickety thing was just a yank away from freedom.

As she readied herself to finish today's demolition job, the door opened, and in walked Gray, Aspen Cove's resident rock star and the new girl. New being a loose term since Beth had been there for several months.

"Be careful up there. I'd hate to see you fall," Gray said.

"Oh, I've already fallen as low as I can go." She smiled and returned her attention to the shelving. "I've got two bags of Fritos left."

Sitting in the store and watching the world pass her by while she licked her wounds gave her lots of opportunities to study people, and she knew Beth and Gray ate her out of Fritos each week, so she ordered a few more bags.

"How did you know?" Beth asked.

"I've learned to pay attention. It was never a strong suit before, but I'm getting better at it." Being married to Matt Monroe taught her many things. If she'd paid closer attention years ago, she would've seen his complete incompetence and maybe the telltale signs of his affair with her best friend, who was their producer. If only she'd seen what was right in front of her, the top-ranking home improvement show might not have cut her.

"Always good to pay attention." Gray cocked his head. "What are you doing?"

"I'm starting from scratch." That was more truth than lie. She'd come to Aspen Cove for a new beginning. Not only had she lost her job but also her self-confidence and self-respect. Starting over in a place where no one was likely to know her had been a good thing.

The door opened, and in walked a man wearing a suit. She'd seen him a time or two, but he wasn't a resident or a frequent visitor.

Beth grabbed the two bags of Fritos corn chips from the display and murmured something to Gray.

The suited man walked a few steps and stopped at the bottom of her ladder.

"Hey, Mason," Beth said. "I know you're here to meet with my mom, but I think she's going to cancel."

Mason's expression went from flat to frazzled.

"What?" He ran a hand through his hair. "Why didn't she call me?"

Jewel watched the exchange. Perched on the ladder, she had the perfect vantage point, yet it seemed as if her presence went unnoticed.

"Everything just happened today." Beth held up her hand and pointed to the ring that caught the light of the fluorescents hanging from chains like eyesores from the ceiling. They would be the first thing she got rid of when she closed temporarily for renovation. "He asked me to marry him, and I said yes. We don't need two houses, so Mom is going to move into mine."

The mention of a house always piqued her interest. She'd been living in the apartment above the store. The word apartment was generous considering it was a studio with a permanent divider between the bed and the living area. She still couldn't remove the smell of BenGay and cigarette smoke. If she stayed there much longer, her sinuses would clear, but she might get lung cancer.

"Did you say your mom was looking at a house?" Jewel asked, drawing attention to herself. "Where?"

When Mason's eyes narrowed and then dawned with recognition, Jewel's stomach turned. *He knows who I am.*

"Hyacinth." His eyes bore into hers. "You're J—"

Tugging on the shelf, it plummeted like a plane without an engine and dropped to the ground. She thought she could control the trajectory, but it slipped from her grip, whacking Mason over his head, sending him to a heap on the linoleum floor.

"Oh, damn," Jewel said. "Maybe I haven't hit rock bottom yet."

"Shall we get Doc?" Beth asked.

Mason held his hand in the air. "Nope, I'm good."

"Are you sure?" Gray rushed forward to help.

Jewel looked at Mason like *he'd* fallen from the sky and not the wooden shelf.

"Yep." He glanced at Jewel and gave his head a shake. "What should I call you?"

"Jewel. I'm Jewel." She held on to the ladder. She should've rushed down to see how serious his injury was, but she was frozen in place. He recognized her, which scared the hell out of her.

Jewel wasn't ready to face the public again. Not only had she been humiliated on television, but the executive producers spun a story to paint her as the bad guy. It was worse than the time Martha Stewart went to prison.

"Right..." Mason's skeptical tone dropped an octave.

"Can I pay for these?" Gray took the chip bags from Beth and held them up. "It's part of the dowry I promised my future wife."

Jewel waved them off. "Consider it an engagement gift." She finally descended the ladder and offered Mason a hand. Once he stood, all three stared, and she smiled even though her innards were twisting like a Twizzler when she said, "Have a great day."

Gray peered at her for the briefest of moments before placing his hand on the small of Beth's back and leading her toward the door.

"So, Jewel?" Mason said. "Care to tell me why you're hiding?"

Her heart pumped so fast, her head spun, and she had to reach for the wall for balance.

"Maybe *you* should have a seat." Mason took her by the hand and ushered her to a stool behind the counter.

On it was one of her lists. She glanced at the title scribbled at the top: 50 *Things you can do with a hammer.* The first entry read *Break Matt's windshield.*

"Bitter much?" Mason raised a brow.

She closed her eyes and took a deep breath as she flopped onto the stool. "Bitter doesn't begin to describe it." She crumpled the paper and tossed it into the nearby trash can. "Look, I'd appreciate it if you kept my location a secret. Half of Matt's newfound solo success comes from slandering me. They call it humor, but I call it torture."

"I'd call it a lawsuit."

She leaned her back against the nearby wall and sighed.

"Pick and choose your battles. That's one I'd never win. They have the resources to bury me."

He chuckled. "They didn't need resources. They used public opinion, and you allowed them to. Never let anyone tell you who you are."

She'd been talking to the man for several minutes but hadn't taken a good look at him. He was stunning with his dark hair and blue eyes. She rarely liked his type, but her kind hadn't proven a wise choice since the last go-around.

"And who are you, Mason?" She pushed some hair from her eyes.

He wiped his hand on what had to be a thousand-dollar suit and offered it to her. "I'm Mason Van der Veen."

She recognized the name. People in small towns murmured loudly, and they had nothing nice to say about him.

"You're the slimy real estate agent?"

Her words didn't seem to chip at his exterior. His look was still one of pure confidence, and his hand remained in place, waiting for a shake.

"Again, never let anyone tell you who you are."

She shook his hand, hoping it didn't make her want to run upstairs and take a shower—it didn't. His grip was firm and his skin warm. Usually a fan of a workingman's hands, it surprised her to find that the softness of his didn't detract from the strength.

"Tell me, is it true?" she asked.

"The real estate agent part or the slimy part?"

She tried to hold the laugh back, but the way his brows lifted to his hairline was comical. It bubbled up and came out sounding like she choked.

He patted her back until she stopped.

"You don't seem all that slimy. Unless you're going to walk out the door and call your lawyer to sue me for whacking you on the head."

"Now that's an idea. How much do you think I could get?"

He was the one who got injured, but it was her brain that ached. She slid from the stool.

"Maybe you should sit. I think you got brain damage when the shelf came down." She spread her arms as if displaying a prize on a game show. "Look around you. This is all I've got. Help yourself to anything."

He took the seat, rubbing the knot on his forehead. "Tell you what, how about I get a water and a couple of painkillers, and we call it a day?"

She narrowed her eyes. "That's all you want?"

He gazed past her and pointed at a display shelf. "And those Raspberry Zingers."

"You're cheap." She walked to the cooler to get his water and snapped up the treats on the way back. Under the counter, she had a large bottle of Tylenol for the daily headaches she endured thinking about her ex-husband.

"Maybe, but I'm not easy."

"At this moment, I wouldn't call you a slimeball."

He opened the water and tossed back two painkillers before taking a drink. "It's just someone's opinion. Are you a hard-ass, ball-busting, talentless hanger-oner who screwed up on a load-bearing wall?"

"Oh my God! You've seen the show."

He opened the Zingers and pulled out the first cake. "It was my favorite." He rocked his head from side to side but winced, mostly likely because of the walnut-sized bump she put there. "I watched a few episodes after you left, but it wasn't the same. You brought something to the show that hasn't been matched."

"Talent?"

"Is it true? You were the brains, and he was the brawn?"

"I was everything. He was beefcake."

"And I thought he was the cake, and you were the icing. Just another pretty face to boost ratings."

*Pretty face? He definitely has a brain injury.*

Mason glanced around the store. "It's hard for me to believe you when you're sitting in a shithole that looks like it hasn't been updated since Kennedy was president."

Shoulders shaking, she said, "More like Eisenhower. I found one of Mamie's hats in the back room. It was a pink number with a flower bigger than my head."

"Seriously, why Aspen Cove?"

"I stopped for a soda and heard the owners talking about selling. I was having an existential moment and needed a purpose."

"And Raspberry Zingers and Fritos called to you?"

A *pffft* sound sputtered from her lips. "No, Fritos are Gray and Beth's thing." She looked at the wrapper he left on the desk. "Zingers are yours. I needed something more substantial." She glanced at the large container of Red Vines sitting on her desk. "I needed purpose and red licorice."

"This place is a wreck, and someone with your background could've whipped it into shape by now if indeed you were the talent."

She lowered her head. "I didn't want to draw attention to myself."

"Is that why you colored your hair brown?" He took a bite of the Zinger and hummed as if it was the best thing he'd eaten in his entire life.

It wasn't that she'd dyed her hair but stopped getting it highlighted, which made it go from a dirty blonde back to its brown origins.

"Speaking of which, how *did* you recognize me?" No one else knew who she was except maybe Goldie, the town's only social influencer, but the woman never said a word once that look of recognition came and went. Since then, Jewel discounted her purchases because of Goldie's loyalty.

"No one has eyes like yours."

"They're just eyes."

He leaned in as if peering into her soul. Laser-like heat danced across her skin.

"Nope, they're like an afternoon storm. Not quite blue and not quite purple with an outer rim of gray. They can be hard as steel and yet soft as a flower petal."

She smiled. "Hyacinth?"

"No, that's far too common. Maybe a faded morning glory."

"No, I was asking about the house on Hyacinth."

"It's a piece of junk. Honestly, most of the houses in town are teardowns."

"Sounds like the perfect place for me. I know a little about home repair."

"So, you say." He rubbed his head with a grin.

She almost reached out to wipe the tiny dab of cream filling that stuck to his lip.

"You really want to see it?"

Adrenaline rushed through her as the familiar high she always got before starting a new project had her nodding, and what better venture to start than refurbing her future home?

"I need to see it." That's what this had become. She needed to smell the fresh-cut pine of two-by-fours and feel the comfortable weight of a hammer in her hand as much as she needed her next breath.

"I have lots of homes to sell. There's even a bridge I've got in Brooklyn that could use a buyer too."

"Stop being slimy. When can you show me the property?"

"How about the day after tomorrow?"

"Deal. Now get out of my store. I've got lists to create."

He moved toward the door, laughing. "I'd take death by shelving off your list. It's not effective."

"Maybe I should get a gun."

"Yeah, probably, but wait until after I show you the houses. I'd hate to be your primary target."

"Impossible, you haven't done me wrong ... yet." She watched that custom-suit-clad man walk out of the store. She wasn't sure what she thought about Mason Van der Veen. Even though he was a real estate agent, which was about the same as being a used car salesman or a politician, he also thought she was a poser, so the scales tipped against him. However, there was something she liked, too. Maybe it was simply that he left.

She grabbed a piece of paper and a pen and started on a new list.

*Reasons to dislike Mason Van der Veen.*

At the top, she wrote, *He looks good in a suit.*

# CHAPTER TWO

Today was a three-sugar day. Typically, Mason didn't take any, but there were times where life's bitter edge required sweetening, and he needed reinforcements.

"Mason, I'm waiting." His father, Trenton Van der Veen, wasn't a patient man, and the irritated tone he greeted Mason with meant he was even less so than his usually irascible self today.

"I'll be there in a second." He stirred his coffee and set the spoon aside.

"Now," his father growled, sending several people sitting in the break room running for cover.

Not willing to hop to his father's bidding, or maybe dreading the outcome of this meeting, Mason took his time. He leaned against the counter and sipped the syrupy brew he concocted.

He knew what the morning meeting was about—his failure to sell the properties in Aspen Cove. It didn't matter that he'd sold several of the dumps. Elite Properties was sitting with ten redheaded stepchildren in its portfolio because he believed Stephen Tobler from the Sterling Group. They were confident they'd scoop up the waterfront property and turn the town into a tourist mecca. Mason convinced his father and the board to invest in Aspen Cove. What a bust that had been. Stephen couldn't get Bea Bennett's property, and that buried the entire plan.

The only saving grace was Mason didn't buy all the properties since Wes Covington picked up quite a few of them, which he seemed to sell well.

Mason kicked off the counter and shuffled toward the conference room like he was walking to the gallows.

His father sat at the end of the large table as if he were a king with his serfs flanking his sides. Mason used to sit at his father's right like a prince, but these days Dad relegated him to standing like a pauper begging for scraps.

"Update."

There were no niceties, no please, no hello, and no how was your trip to Aspen Cove? It was all business.

"I didn't sell the property on Hyacinth." Months

ago, he would've hung his head in shame, but disappointment was where he resided. He couldn't sink lower than the gum on his father's shoe.

"Of course not. You probably couldn't give them away. Hell, you almost did with that last one. Why in the world would you agree to finance the property?"

His father was talking about Beth Buchanan.

"I sold it. That was the aim, right?" He moved farther into the room where the wall of windows overlooked downtown Denver. "She's making the payments."

"Profit is the objective. We didn't go into this venture to make pennies on the dollar. If you can't deliver, we'll have to replace you."

Mason swallowed the lump in his throat. He was sure if his dad could wipe the Van der Veen DNA from his body, he would.

His shoulders sagged. "Do what you have to do." He wasn't married to Aspen Cove, and if his father thought another person could move the properties, he'd gladly stand aside.

His dad stood, and at six feet four, he towered over most men. Mason wasn't an exception, but at least his six-foot frame didn't have him looking up at his father. He was always eye to nose—close enough.

"I will. You have sixty days to get a plan in place. If you haven't moved twenty percent of the homes by then, you're fired." His father cleared his throat and leaned in so only Mason could hear him deliver the final blow. "And disowned."

Being fired was one thing, but disowned was another. Who was he, if not a Van der Veen? He'd still carry the name, but his father would make sure he forfeited all the privileges, including his family-owned car, penthouse, and trust fund.

"I've got a plan." He thought about Jewel or JJ Monroe as he knew her on the show. "I'm working out a deal to feature the homes on a DIY show." He hated to lie, but he needed time to figure out a real strategy. "If I can land the star, then maybe we can get the homes refurbished for free, and Elite Properties would benefit from the publicity."

His dad lifted his brows. "Who's the star?"

Leave it to his father to demand a name. "Does it matter?"

"Yes."

Mason stared past his dad at the table of men who nodded like bobbleheads. There wasn't a leader in the group. His dad's followers were nothing more than minions, and he had been one of them—still was. He didn't have a choice until he could break away, but that was impossible when his father was the powerful Trenton Van der Veen. His father ate hubcaps for breakfast and spit nails for dinner.

"I have nothing locked up."

The red glow started just above his father's tie

and bloomed like fast-moving lava into his receding hairline.

"Don't you come in here and tell me about a grand scheme you haven't even negotiated. Those types of deals don't happen overnight. They take months to plan and implement."

It was an off-the-cuff idea, but it had merit. His brief conversation with Jewel told him more than he needed to know. She was bitter, and if she was indeed the talent, they had mistreated her. If he were her, he'd want revenge served on prime-time television, but his father was right, deals like that took preparation and planning, and all he had was sixty days.

"I'll turn two of the houses, but I'll need money to refurbish. I can't sell a house without a floor or one without a ceiling. Could you invest slightly more to move the process along?" He stepped back, hoping not to get splashed with the brain matter that seemed ready to explode from his father's beet-red head.

"No, of course not," Trenton said in an uncharacteristically singsong voice. "How about we finance them all? Let's fix all those houses and give them away as a sign of goodwill."

His voice rose until Mason was sure the windows shook.

"That's a no then."

"You know what? I'm giving you a break today.

Pick two houses, and I'll make them yours. I'll even give you the money to refurb the first one."

Gasps from the minion's table filled the air. All it took was a well-placed glare from his father to silence them.

"You will?"

His father smiled. It wasn't an I'm-helping-you-out smile, but an I'm-giving-you-enough-rope-to-hang-yourself smirk.

"Let's call it an early inheritance."

That set off alarms that rang so loudly in Mason's head he was sure his eardrums would burst.

He moved closer to his father and whispered, "You're releasing my trust?"

In a laugh that could rival Santa, he patted Mason on the back. "No, son, I'm releasing you."

"You're disowning me?"

"It's time you manned up or got out. I've been carrying you for thirty-four years. It's time for you to make your mark on the world. You'll never do that if I'm dragging you around on my coattails."

"Meeting adjourned." His father turned to the others. "We will fairly compensate you for this transaction. I'll pay you from Mason's trust fund."

They scurried like mice until the only two left were him and his father. "You're taking my trust fund away completely?" Mason's heart raced like a Maserati on a test track.

"I'm trading assets. You get two houses and a hundred grand to start your pie-in-the-sky scheme. I'll keep the thirty million from your trust. Sable wants to go to the Maldives."

"Sable? Your masseuse?"

His father licked his lips and smiled. "She's got amazing hands."

"I bet, but seriously, you're taking everything away?"

"It's time to prove your worth."

Mason staggered back. "What about when I brought you the Piper deal? Three downtown blocks of prime real estate for a steal. You made half of my trust in that deal alone. I proved my worth then."

His father straightened his tie. "Prove you're not a one-trick pony. Create something out of nothing, and I'll hand over your inheritance."

This was pure manipulation. Mason was due to inherit his trust fund the day he turned thirty-five, only two months away. This wasn't about the property in Aspen Cove. It was only a method of delivering his father's message. This was about control and Trenton's reminder that Mason would never have any.

His father left him staring out the window at the Rockies. The big, majestic mountains that held the key to his future. Surely, he could turn around a couple of houses to appease good old Dad. To most people, losing ten bucks was problematic, but thirty million ... that was life-changing ... life-ending, really.

Rather than stay in the office, Mason bought a latte from the ground-level barista and headed to his penthouse blocks away. He had the next few weeks to plan. His hundred grand wouldn't get him far. If Jewel was as good as she said, he needed to get on her good side because she could be an asset.

His pace picked up as he walked toward his home, but his heart stumbled and hit the cement when he saw Dan the doorman glance at him with a frown. Or maybe it was the moving truck sitting open and his couch in the center that spurred the panic attack.

He rushed forward. "What the heck is happening?"

"You've been evicted." Dan pulled an envelope from his pocket and handed it to Mason. "Your father had this delivered moments ago. The truck arrived not long before. He says you'll need to tell the movers where to take your stuff." Dan walked away, leaving Mason standing there with his mouth agape.

He tore open the envelope. In the end, Trenton Van der Veen would decide. He gave him the deeds to two properties and a check for a hundred grand. On his letterhead, there was a note. All it said was *Go forth and multiply*. He wasn't talking procreation.

Nope, he was talking dollars. If Mason failed to turn this into something more, then all he'd have was two teardown properties and a check for what he spent on suits a year.

"Damn it."

"Sir," the mover said. "Where is this going?"

Mason looked at the list of properties his father gave him. He closed his eyes and pointed, and when he opened them again, his finger was on Hyacinth. The house next door to the one Jewel wanted to see tomorrow.

"You can deliver here."

He remembered little about the property, but he knew it wasn't the one with a hole in the floor and a rodent problem.

He walked toward the entrance, but Dan shook his head. "Sorry, man, you can't come in."

"Are you serious?"

"I need this job. The wife is pregnant again, and the oldest needs braces."

With a sigh, Mason held out his hand. "Can I at least have the keys to my car, or did he repossess that too?"

"I'll bring it around." Dan pulled the keys to his Mercedes SUV from the cabinet. "Stay here, okay?"

"You got it." People might have thought he was slimy because he tried to sell subpar housing at premium prices, but seeing Dan's daughter's teeth, even he wouldn't risk her opportunity at orthodontia.

A few minutes later, the doorman pulled in front of the building. "Good luck, sir."

Mason walked toward the driver's side. "I'm going to need it."

He had a three-hour drive to devise a plan. How was he going to get his life back?

# CHAPTER THREE

Hunched over the kitchen table, Jewel studied her finances once more. The Corner Store was profitable. It paid its bills and then some. She'd never be able to buy an island or a yacht, but she was landlocked in Colorado, so it didn't much matter. Those weren't on her bucket list, anyway.

Taped to her refrigerator was her immediate goal list.

*Eat less licorice.*

*Exercise*

*Stop making lists*

That would be the hardest to accomplish because for as long as she could remember, she'd created them. By the time she was ten, she had her life planned down to the Yorkie puppy and the color of her husband's boxer briefs. There would be no tighty whiteys in her home.

She closed her computer and sighed. She could afford a house if the price was right—it would be tight but doable.

Nine months post-divorce and she still couldn't figure out where her and Matt's money had gone. It wasn't like they made a ton, but they should've had more than they did. They traveled for *Reno or Wreck It,* so the show covered most of their expenses. While they weren't making the money A-list actors pulled in, it wasn't a minimum wage job either.

It was senseless to allow her ex to consume her thoughts. She knew she needed to forgive him because all this anger and hatred was making her bitter. Nothing affected him. Why would it? He had a job and a fiancée as well as an intact reputation. The heat of anger rose once again, but the sound of the bell on the door downstairs meant she had a customer and couldn't blaze for too long.

She opened the door that led to the store. "Be right down."

"Take your time. I'm just looking at your latest list."

She recognized the voice, and panic sliced through her. *What list did I leave on the desk?*

"You stay out of my stuff." She raced down the stairs, and when she turned the corner, she came face-to-face with Mason, who had a piece of paper in his hand and a grin on his face.

He laid it down on the counter. "You think I look good in a suit, and that's a reason to hate me?" He shook his head. "I'm wondering about you." He glanced around the store. "Award-winning builder lives in a rundown apartment above the country store."

She fisted her hips. "It's *The Corner Store,* and how do you know it's run down?"

"Have you refurbed it since you moved in?" He walked to the pastry display and picked up a package of Raspberry Zingers, then moved down the cooler aisle and opened the door to get a soda.

"I cleaned it. It took me a week to scrape off the years of grime collected while Phillip and Marge lived there."

"The place is a college dorm room at best—a jail cell at worst."

She had to agree with him. It felt like she was serving a sentence. It was probably a life term for being so trusting, with an extra five years added for being stupid.

"Sounds like you've seen it."

He popped the tab on the can and took a drink.

"I was listing it when you bopped on in here and made a side deal. I lost a good commission because of you."

She moved to the register. "And now somehow I owe you?" She rang him up.

He pulled out his wallet and gave her a five. "No, apparently I owe you."

"That's the way I like it." She lifted on her tiptoes and stared down at his jeans. "Casual for the hard sell you're going to give me."

Last night she drove by the house on Hyacinth. There were two, side by side, and they were both in awful shape but had potential.

"Nothing I do is hard." He tore into the Zinger wrapper and took a bite.

"That's a shame. I'm sure there's a string of disappointed women." She couldn't believe she said that to him. She was always bold, but never that bold. When she went back upstairs, she'd need to add lobotomy to her list. Maybe if they took out her frontal lobes, she'd get into less trouble.

He choked on his cupcake. "Except that. That's hard." He frowned and shook his head. "I don't mean it's hard now or hard to do. I'm very good at it. No string of disappointed women left behind."

She watched as he squirmed. It was fun to watch Mr. Expensive Suit, who gets hundred-dollar haircuts and wears sexy smelling cologne, get nervous.

"Doesn't matter to me. I'm not interested. The only thing you're good for is a house." She grabbed her keys from the desk and walked to the front of the store. "Shall we go?"

"Don't I get change?" The look she gave him made him drop the question and pick up his stuff to follow her out of the store.

After she locked up, she faced him.

"Your car, my car, or walk."

By his expression, she was confident that Mason walked nowhere.

"Let's walk."

Her wide eyes and open mouth told him his decision floored her. "You want to walk?"

He looked at the blue sky. "It's a beautiful afternoon, and the sun's out. Why not? You think I don't walk anywhere?"

She gave him another glance before she headed down Main Street toward the turn to Hyacinth. He held himself like a silver spoon, spoiled aristocrat, but there was something down-to-earth about him too. He was this fascinating mix of *The Fresh Prince of Bel-Air* meets *Schitt's Creek*.

"Nice jeans."

He looked down at his tattered Levi's and smiled. "You like them?"

She laughed. "Yes, they go well with your driving moccasins."

They turned down Rose Lane and kept walking.

"If you think making fun of my clothes is going to get you a better deal, you're wrong."

"I wouldn't think of it. You'll need every penny to buy your next pair. What do those cost?"

He frowned. "I'm not telling you."

"Italian leather?"

"Let's not talk about my clothes. How about I tell you about the house on Hyacinth?"

She moved to the right of the sidewalk so he could catch up and walk next to her.

"How about *I* tell you about it?"

He cocked his head and looked at her. Taking his eyes off the uneven sidewalk was a mistake because he hit a lift in the cement and fell forward. Thankfully, she was quick and strong and could stop him from hitting the ground.

Once he righted himself, he stopped and gawked at her. "Geez, woman. I swear you're out to get me."

"Me? I'm not the one who wore driving shoes. I'm not the one who took my eyes off the ground. I'm not the one who ... who—"

"Who what?"

Her skin prickled the way it did when she touched a live wire. It should've been an unpleasant feeling, but somehow, sparring with Mason made her feel alive for the first time in a long time.

"Who stood under a ladder? Haven't you heard those old wives' tales? Never let a black cat cross your path. Eating before bed causes nightmares, and never walk under a ladder."

"I didn't," he said and moved forward. "I stood next to the ladder. It wasn't the ladder that brought me bad luck. It was you. I almost think you let the shelf fall on my head just to shut me up."

*She wondered that too.* "I'd never do that on purpose. Although it worked, so I might have to add it to my list labeled, *How to shut someone up.*"

"I don't know why you're so keen on keeping your identity a secret."

"You said you saw the show, right? I removed a load-bearing wall, and the room fell in on itself on national television. The crew scrambled to get out, and when the dust settled, my career was over."

They turned the corner and were at the house.

"Why is that? Why did you remove that wall?"

"Because I wasn't thorough. I asked Matt to go over the plans and reconfirm with the inspector that the wall was safe to move, and he said he did, but he didn't."

"Where was he in all this?"

"Balls deep in the producer."

He snapped his mouth shut.

She was getting some actual skill at shutting people up. "Shall we go in?"

He reached his hand into his pocket. "I was sure I brought the key. I can—"

"The back door is unlocked." She moved through the chain-link gate and stepped up to the back door. If she bought this dump, she was putting down pavers for an outdoor living space come summer.

"You broke in here last night?"

She rolled her eyes. It was such a juvenile thing to do, but some scenarios called for it. "No, I walked in the unlocked back door. I told you I could tell you about this house."

"Okay then, tell me why you should buy this house?"

A giggle started in her spleen and rose to her throat. "I shouldn't, but since there are few homes that are habitable, then I suppose this house or the one next door are my options."

He shook his head. "Nope, the one next door isn't available."

She gave him a quiet-on-the-set look. "You sold it?"

"No, I'm living there. It's a long story."

"You're living in that hellhole? It's worse than this place."

"You went in there too?"

She shrugged. "You should lock the doors."

"This is Aspen Cove." He stepped inside the house and flipped on the switch, but the lights didn't come on.

"The breaker box is shot."

"Tell me what I don't know."

She moved into the living room. "No way, you tell me what I want to know. How in the hell did you come to live in Aspen Cove since our meeting the day before yesterday? Are you brain damaged?"

He touched the bruise on his forehead. "Maybe. I got hit with a shelf."

# CHAPTER FOUR

Mason had a choice to make at this moment. Did he come clean and tell her the truth, that his father disowned him and he had one last chance to prove himself? Or did he lie and tell her he wanted to be close to his work?

"I got evicted." The truth was always a better path to travel.

She frowned and rubbed her chin. "I thought you were some real estate mogul."

He laughed. "Elite Properties does well. It's a family business, but Aspen Cove hasn't been the boon I thought it would be. I made a business decision, and it didn't turn out well. Disowning me is the penalty."

She gasped. "Your family disowned you?" Her

mouth dropped open, then snapped shut. "Geez, I don't think that's the family I'd want to be a part of."

He walked into the kitchen, straight out of an *I Love Lucy* set, with its free-standing white stove and yellowed, painted cabinets. The refrigerator was missing, but the cutout for it was there.

"We don't get to choose our family."

She ran her hand over the chipped surface of the stove. "Not true. You can't choose who you're born to, but you certainly can choose who you decide to make a family with. I chose poorly."

He realized he knew little about her, and something inside him wanted to learn more. "How about I take you to lunch?"

"Are you going to give me the hard sell on the house?"

"Of course, it's what I do. Are you going to low-ball me on an offer?"

She headed toward the back door. "I'd be stupid not to."

"It's obvious you're not stupid."

"Oh, I have my moments. I married Matt, didn't I?"

He followed her out the back. "Do you want me to lock the door to your house?"

"Look at you trying to emotionally connect me to the place by calling it my house."

"It's yours if you want it."

"We'll see."

They walked side by side in silence. How to get his trust fund reinstated filled his thoughts. Hers were probably already working on which room to gut first.

"Tell me, where will you start?"

She looked up at him with those crazy blue eyes. Today they seemed more tropical, like seeing the house or the possibility of having a project brought color to their usual stormy blue. He didn't think he'd ever seen them filled with such passion.

"I think a salad and then a burger," she stated as she turned onto Main Street.

"You know what I mean."

"Yes, and I'm not letting you work your hocus pocus and get me invested in the house bullshit before we discuss terms."

At the corner where the Sheriff's Station stood, they crossed the street and went into the diner.

No matter what time he entered, it always smelled like bacon and maple syrup. It reminded him of his childhood. Ideally, it should've been one of his parents serving up breakfast on a Saturday morning, but it was Heidi, their German housekeeper, who always made him bacon and eggs served with hard rolls and a jar of Nutella.

"Booth or table?" He looked around and saw both were open but knew it wouldn't be long before the dinner crowd showed up because Maisey's filled up at each mealtime.

"I prefer a booth."

He led her to the one by the window. "Me too. Unless you're the one trapped on the inside and can't get out. Booths also suck when you're at a buffet."

"You feel trapped often?"

He hadn't considered his life a trap, but honestly, it was. He was a pawn in the Van der Veen chess game.

"No," he lied.

"You go to buffets often?" She lifted a perfectly plucked brow. "You don't seem like the Country Buffet kind of guy."

"They have the best chicken-fried chicken ever." He hoped that was one of their dishes because he'd never been to a buffet in his life.

"Whoever is telling you that someone has a better chicken-fried chicken than me, they're lying." Maisey had snuck up on them and rested her hip on the end of the booth bench. "Is that what you're having?"

He chuckled. "Yep, let me be the judge."

Maisey made a sound of disbelief. "How about you, Jewel? You want the same?"

"Oh no, I'm having a bacon cheeseburger and a salad with Italian dressing. And a root beer as well."

Mason smiled. "I'll have a root beer too."

He glanced at Jewel and saw the dimples in the corners of her mouth. She was stunning when she smiled.

"I'll get that order in before all hell breaks loose. It's Wednesday, and you know what that means." Maisey turned and left.

Mason didn't know what Wednesday meant in Aspen Cove. "What did she mean?"

After an indulgent giggle at his expense. "You know nothing about this town, do you?"

"Not true."

She leaned in and rested her elbows on the table. "Okay, Mr. Smarty Pants, tell me what you know."

"It was a boomtown about fifty years ago. Settled by three families about a hundred years ago, including the Guilds," His heart ached when he thought of his lost friendship with Wes Covington, who was a Guild on his mother's side of the family. There was a disagreement on a property they were co-developing. Wes's father's architecture firm designed it, and Mason's father was supposed to develop the property. Things went wrong, and the two families battled it out in court. The Van der Veens won and that ended all ties to the Covingtons. He'd stayed loyal to his family, and that seemed always to cost him everything, including his best friend.

"Go on."

Maisey trotted by, dropping off their drinks before she moved on to the next table to arrive—a group of women who looked out of place in their heels and miniskirts.

"The paper factory went under, and the town languished until some pop star bought the old building and turned it into something."

She flopped back into the booth. "Some pop star? Are you kidding me?" She picked up her soda and took a gulp. "Her name is Indigo." Her shoulders shook with laughter. "It's Samantha, but the band is called Indigo. She isn't just some pop star. She's *the* pop star, and the Guild Creative Center isn't just any place. It's the place for anything artistic. It houses some of the finest artisans in Colorado, maybe the country."

He lifted his shoulders. "Okay, so tell me what that has to do with Wednesdays."

"Look around you."

He glanced slowly around the perimeter of the diner and tried to see what she was seeing, but all he saw was lipstick, miles of bare legs, and shoes high enough to make a podiatrist cry.

"I don't understand."

"It's karaoke night at Bishop's Brewhouse."

"And that means something because?"

"Because the band always takes part. It gives the fans a way to connect to the members while they aren't touring. Samantha and Deanna are pregnant, so no tours for the next few years."

He took in the clientele again and realized there wasn't a local in the place. "Wow, I'm really not paying attention."

"No, and you could've been using this to your advantage. Put a card in each of these girls' hands and tell them how far they could live from the band members. It's like being in Hollywood and handing people a map to the stars. Who wouldn't want to live next to George Clooney?"

He raised his hand. "Me. He does nothing for me."

"You know what I mean."

He had to give her credit. Sometimes selling something simply came to the effectiveness of the campaign.

"While we're discussing property, what do I have to do to get you to buy the one on Hyacinth?"

"Give it to me." She moved her straw around the glass and watched the ice cubes swirl.

"I can't. I have to sell it and for a profit."

Maisey whizzed by and dropped off their food. "If you say this isn't the best you've ever had, I'll buy it, but I'll know you're lying."

"I'm sure you're right." He moved the plate so the chicken was on the right, the mashed potatoes on the left, and the green beans were on top. He didn't know why he did it, but he'd always eaten his meals like this. "Now, back to the house."

She forked a cherry tomato and held it in the air. "If you want more than a hundred grand, you're nuts."

He'd taken a bite and nearly choked. "Anything less than two, and I'm screwed."

"I guess we have little to discuss then." She popped the tomato into her mouth. After she swallowed, she said, "How is that chicken-fried chicken?"

"The best I've ever had." He took another bite. "Are we going to sit here and chat about the meal?"

"We have nothing else to talk about. You want a premium price for a low-grade property. It would probably be cheaper to bulldoze it and start over."

"You'd never do that." He knew for a fact that she loved the bones of a property. In one of her episodes, she said she could hear the walls talk to her and tell her the home's life story. "What do you think the house would say if it could talk to you?"

She nibbled away at her burger, but he could see by the rapid blinking of her eyes and the sound of her foot tapping under the table that she was thinking.

"I'd say it was telling me to run."

"Now who's lying? You and I both know that you don't run from a wreck that needs a remodel."

She narrowed her eyes at him. "You're good and have done your homework. That's one of my mottos."

"No, I'm a fan."

Her shoulders shook with her fake laugh. "A fan of a woman you're not even sure is the talent on the show." She picked up her napkin and wiped her mouth. "Those are your words, not mine."

He couldn't argue with her. He had, on more than one occasion, questioned her skill set. "Prove it."

"You won't challenge me into a shitty purchase. Contrary to popular belief, just because you're on television doesn't mean you're rich. I own a corner store that barely makes ends meet, and it also needs refurbishing. In fact, I'm closing for the rest of the week starting tomorrow so that I can give it a little facelift."

"Fine. But don't forget it was you who showed an interest in the property initially. I didn't walk into the store begging you to see what I offered."

"You're right, but now I see what you're offering is far below what I'm used to."

Change the location and person he was talking to, and it could've been a conversation he had with his father.

"I always seem to come up short."

She studied for him for a second. The rigid set of her jaw seemed to soften.

"This isn't personal."

"Yeah, well, you don't know me, and this feels

personal. I stand to lose or gain everything from selling or not selling those two houses."

She reached into her back pocket and pulled out a twenty and set it on the table. "Then I'd say, go home and get more cards. You're going to have a busy night at the Brewhouse. Where else can you get a roomful of hungry buyers who want what you're offering?"

"They might want it, but can they afford it?"

"Never judge a groupie by her heels." She slid out of the booth. "It's the ones who shop at Payless or Kohl's that probably have a nest egg. In my experience, sensible crosses the lines from shopping to life choices."

"Says the woman who bought a corner store on a whim."

"I've made bigger mistakes in my life. At least this one won't sleep with the delivery person."

She turned and walked away.

His life wasn't any different than it had been that morning, but it felt so much worse like somehow he'd finally hit rock bottom.

# CHAPTER FIVE

It had been three days since she closed the store to work on it and five since she'd seen Mason. She moved around the empty building, wondering how she wanted to put it all back together.

Painted in a warm beige, the walls almost appeared to say thank you after living with soiled stark white for years.

She wanted to give Sherwin Williams a standing ovation for having the perfect shade to calm her chaotic world. It wasn't just the paint that made a difference. The industrial-strength, laminate floor was also an upgrade. While she would've loved to have put in hardwood, the faux flooring made the place look more country store than a corner store, and it would be maintenance-free and last for years.

A coat of paint on the shelving was like putting jewelry on for a special occasion. A ribbon of pure joy spread through her as she glanced around. She'd dressed up the place with a small budget and a lot of muscle.

It'd been months since she'd done anything besides clean and run the cash register. Using skills she'd honed since childhood working beside her father made her feel whole again.

As she muscled the shelving back into place, she considered her new life in Aspen Cove. She'd mostly kept to herself. In her mind, there was a waiting period between the divorce and the continuation of life. While she was happy to shed the extra weight of an unfaithful husband, he took everything else with him. It felt kind of like those old stories where you hear the wife got the house, the car, and the poodle, except Matt took it all.

"You were stupid." She shoved the first shelving unit into place. "You didn't fight for anything."

That was the problem with being an ostrich. She buried her head in the sand and let life pass her by because pulling her head up and looking around was a dose of reality she wasn't ready to accept until now.

"New day ... new life." Was it sad that she talked to herself all the time, and for entertainment, she wrote lists? Last night was all about the house on Hyacinth. Most people would doze the place, but she could imagine how beautiful it'd be if she restored it. It was a cute bungalow with a lovely front porch. Inside were three decent-sized bedrooms, an enormous living room with a stone fireplace, and a kitchen that needed gutting. While she loved the free-standing stove, it wasn't practical for modern living. There wasn't a piece of counter anywhere in that kitchen to use as a workspace.

She started her list by gutting the kitchen and ended it with the paver stone patio with a built-in fire pit and outdoor kitchen.

Just thinking about it made living in the one-room shanty upstairs nearly unbearable.

As she moved the shelves into their new configuration, she thought about Mason and if he'd sold her home. *Her home.* That was how she thought of the place since she first walked inside. It was like it reached out and hugged her with grimy arms and asked her to save it.

Maybe she walked away to prove that she could but was walking away from her future wise?

"He wants too much."

The list she made the night before had all the reasons Mason Van der Veen was a crook and started with the price of the house and ended with his stupid driving shoes. She didn't know why those bothered her so much, but it was probably because they were such a prig thing to wear.

Would she regret walking away?

Her father's voice sounded in her head: *It's better to look forward with optimism than look back with regret.*

Then her mother's voice came with: *daylights a-wastin'.*

"You need some help with those?"

Startled, she spun to face Mason.

"How did you get in here?"

He chuckled. "Seems as if you're picking up some Aspen Cove habits because you left the back door unlocked."

She gripped on to the shelving like it was the only thing keeping her standing. With her heart racing, it probably was.

"You nearly gave me a heart attack." She let go of one hand and placed it on her chest—the thud of her heartbeat pounded against the cage that held it. "What are you doing here?"

He rocked back and forth on his hiking boots. *Hiking boots?*

"I'm craving a package of Zingers."

She walked to the next unit that needed moving. "We're closed."

"I know, but I thought since we're friends, you'd make an exception."

"We're friends?"

He shrugged. "We could be."

"Well, if you were truly a friend, you'd get the other side of that shelf and help me move it."

He did as she asked, and a job that would have taken another hour if she were alone only took them thirty minutes to finish.

"Changing the configuration?"

She walked to the box next to the milk cooler and pulled out a package of Zingers.

"I don't know what they were thinking, but it wasn't a friendly atmosphere, and it was dangerous. Once someone got down the first aisle, I couldn't see them." She pointed to the big dome mirror mounted in the corner. "With the aisles opening toward the door, I can see what everyone is up to."

"You're pretty and smart."

That was the second time he called her pretty.

"In my experience, requests always followed flattery, so what do you need?"

He glanced at the Raspberry Zinger in her hand.

"Let's start with that."

She tossed it to him before she moved toward the new counter. It was amazing what she could whip up with a circular saw and a few pieces of wood.

"You sell the house yet?"

He tore the wrapper and took a bite like a starving animal. She was partial to Ding Dongs herself, but the Zingers weren't bad and sold well.

"Nope, I handed my cards out as you said, and

later that night, I got three calls asking if I wanted to stand in for Red."

"No sale, but a bunch of booty calls. Did you take any of them up on their offer?"

It wasn't her business, but she wanted to know.

"Of course not." He raised the last bite of his treat. "I'm cheap, but I'm not easy."

Why that sent a feeling of relief through her system, she couldn't say, but knowing he hadn't hooked up with the first girl who offered, made her like him more.

"So now what?"

"I came to negotiate a deal with you."

Every cell in her body jolted to life. Even her ears were ringing.

"What?"

"A deal." He looked around the store and smiled. "It appears you were the talent."

She laughed. "And don't forget, I have a pretty face." She tossed his earlier sentiments back, hoping that he took them as she meant, which was a dose of humor in an awkward situation.

"I'll never forget that face." He smiled as if he were smitten, but she knew lots of men like Mason. They could charm the panties off of a nun. "But it's not your face I'm here to talk about."

"No, you said you have a deal to discuss."

He pointed to the old stool she had yet to paint.

"Do you care if I sit?" Before she could answer, he pulled it next to hers. "Have a seat, and I'll get started."

"Sounds serious." She watched him reach for her notepad and pen.

He moved through the pages until he got to a blank one. "Glad to see you haven't found another reason to hate me."

"Or there are plenty. I just haven't returned to that list." Her eyes went to his shoes. "See, you upgraded your footwear."

He stuck his foot out and turned it back and forth as if modeling the boots. "These are a downgrade as far as price and comfort, but a necessity for construction. They have steel toes, and I hear that's important."

She stuck her foot out, tapping his with her black work boot. "Imperative. Safety first."

"Unless you're dealing with load-bearing walls." He smiled as if he were teasing, and she saw a glint of light dance in his eyes.

She took the notebook and turned it to the *Reasons to dislike Mason* list, and added:

*Has poor timing and delivery.* In the following line, she wrote. *Poor taste in shoes.* She dropped to the next line. *Doesn't know when to shut up.*

He grabbed the pen from her and crossed out all the lines and put, *Has a wicked sense of humor.*

*Makes incredible lasagna. Desperately needs your help.*

He set the pen down and stared at her. He looked like one of those sad hound dogs begging with his eyes. If she had a milk bone, she would have given him one.

"What do you need from me?"

He took in a big breath and let it out. "Everything."

He explained what was at stake for him if he didn't turn the houses and then sat there for a few minutes.

She half expected him to offer to pay her back once he got his trust, but he didn't.

"Mason, I understand the predicament you're in, but I don't see how I can help you. I'm still not paying for a diamond when I'm getting glass. It's bad business, and you of all people should know that."

He nodded. "I do, which is why I've come up with something else that will help both of us. You need a home and a purpose and possibly a way to get back at your ex. I need to sell some houses."

She sat taller, as if that would help her hear.

All three things appealed to her. "I'm all ears."

He turned the notebook to the blank page and drew out some kind of Venn diagram with bubbles connecting.

His name was in one, and hers was in another.

He connected and drew an arrow down to a partnership.

"Here's what I'm thinking. I'll sell you the house
for what I paid for it."

She nearly jumped from her seat. "You will?"

He wrote the amount down and underlined it
three times.

"Oh my God, you were trying to bamboozle me."

"No, I was being a smart businessman and capi-
talizing on my investment. A property is only worth
what someone will pay for it."

She stared down at the five-figure total. "And
you're willing to sell it to me for this?"

"On one condition."

She slid from the stool and walked to the cooler.
"I need a drink. You want a beer?"

"You got Stella?"

"No, but I've got Bud."

"I'll take it, but maybe I should start a list on you,
and on the top, it'll say has poor taste in beer."

"Do it and see how far that gets us in our negotia-
tions for my house."

"Your house, huh?"

She laughed. "You knew it was, and I knew it was
the minute I snuck inside."

"You mean, broke in and trespassed."

"It was unlocked," she groaned.

"It's all in the details."

She came back with the beer and twisted off the cap to both before she handed him one.

"Now, tell me about this deal."

He cleared his throat. "If I sell you the house at my cost, then at least I've sold it, and my father's stipulation was that I turn these two properties in sixty days. Your house will be a wash. Since he's only given me a hundred grand to refurb both, I figure if I don't have to refurb yours, that gives me the entire amount to work on my place."

"Your place?"

"It's temporary. Believe me, I'm not used to bathing in lukewarm water in a tub with a shower curtain."

She took a drink of her beer. "I bet you've got a fancy steam shower with jets coming from every direction and a rain showerhead."

"When were you in my penthouse?"

She rolled her eyes and wiggled her way back to her seat. "Oh, Mr. Van der Veen, the penthouse?" She said in her best coo, which sounded more like something got stuck in her throat. While she was a girl, she wasn't raised wearing pretty dresses and bows in her hair. Her family was solid working class, and they all worked side by side.

"You can tease, but have you ever been in a luxe shower? It's like having a personal masseuse at the ready twenty-four seven."

"I've been in plenty, but honestly, nothing beats a masseuse. I'd take hands on my body over jets any day." What came out sounded sexual, and that wasn't her intent, but looking at Mason's hands, she imagined they'd been on a lot of bodies during his life.

Feeling a rush of heat on her cheeks, she picked up her beer and took several gulps.

"Touch is always better." He almost purred the words, or that's what it seemed like.

Could words feel like velvet across the skin? Hers tingled from the virtual caress.

"Right," she said breathlessly. "Let's touch on your plan. How do I fit in?" She had a feeling she knew precisely how, but she wanted to hear him say it.

"You're going to help me turn that weed into a flower. I have a limited budget, so I need to do a lot of the labor myself, but I don't know what in the hell I'm doing, so I thought you could get your house cheap, help me restore mine quickly, and in the process if you want we can film the work you're doing and share it. My family is connected, and I'm sure we've got a few media types that would be more than willing to share what you've been up to since you vanished."

Her heart twisted. "No, while I'd love for Matt to step on a rusty nail, I don't want publicity." Panic rose, and so did her voice. "Things are finely dying down. The snide whispers have silenced, and no one is calling me Wreck-It-Rita or Demolition Barbie. No publicity. I vanished because I don't want anyone to find me. Do you have any idea how hard it is to live down a complete blunder like that?"

"I imagine it's as mortifying as having your father disown you and telling the doorman to evict you."

She reached out and laid her hand on top of his. It was a gesture to show she cared, but the touch felt like eating a Snickers bar after a week-long fast. She was starving for connection.

"If you promise not to tell anyone that I'm helping you, then it's a deal."

He offered his hand to shake. "Deal. When can we begin?"

She glanced around the store. "As soon as you help me merchandise the shelves."

"Will you pay me in beer and Zingers?"

"I might even make you a microwave pizza if you're quick."

He hopped off the stool and walked to where she had the can goods boxed in the corner. "You drive a hard bargain, Ms. Monroe."

"You're getting a good deal."

He smiled. "I know."

# CHAPTER SIX

There was no way she could run the store and refurb two houses without help. Getting shit done was her superpower, but even Wonder Woman had her limits.

The door opened and in walked Beth.

"Fritos are in aisle nine," Jewel said.

Beth twirled in a circle, looking at the work she'd done. It was more than paint. With interesting merchandising and the cool wall decals she'd cut on her Cricut, the store took on a sweeter, small-town feel.

"I love what you did with the place."

"Thank you." A sense of pride swelled inside. The most beautiful thing about refurbishing was seeing the fruits of her labor.

She glanced at Beth's growing baby bump and

considered how pregnancy might feel. Having kids was an amazing thing. It wasn't like taking a piece of wood and creating furniture. Making a baby must be the ultimate in DIY projects. You blended two people and came up with a prototype. The problem was you didn't get to see the results for years. Sure, there were smaller markers of success like talking, walking, and report cards. Those were milestones in lives, but the payoff wasn't immediate. Parents didn't truly get to see if their hard work paid off until their kids grew into adulthood.

Beth brought two bags of Fritos to the counter. She groaned and rubbed at her back. "I can't even imagine what this will feel like next month or the month after. Those shifts on my feet all night are killing me."

Jewel rang her up. "You're with a very wealthy man. Why do you work?"

"It gives me purpose."

Boy, Jewel knew how that felt. "I get it."

"I don't want to be a kept woman. I think it's important to be independent."

"I agree," Jewel said as she bagged up the Fritos. She considered her predicament and Beth's. "Hey, are you married to your job at the Brewhouse?"

"God, no. I took it because it was the only job in town. I'm a vet tech, but Charlie doesn't need help because she's got Eden."

Jewel slid the bag forward but didn't let go when Beth went to take it. "Do you want to work here? You can sit behind the counter most days. Even though I took the TV out, I'm willing to bring in a small one, so you have something to do."

Beth cocked her head. "You need help?"

Jewel thought about the homes on Hyacinth. "I've got a project I'm working on, and it's going to take up a lot of my time. I could throw in all the Fritos you can eat as a bonus."

"Let me get this straight. You want me to sit behind your counter and ring up orders while I eat Fritos and watch TV?"

She had considered none of those selling points, but for the right person, it was probably nirvana.

"I guess that sums it up. We're on winter hours, so we're only open from ten to six."

"Wow." Beth reached across the counter. "Pinch me so I know I'm not dreaming. Gray just said how much he didn't like me working at the bar because he worried about the drunk guys. This must be providence."

Jewel wanted to laugh because few people used words like providence, or kismet, or destiny. She put little value in leaving things up to the universe, but then again, there was a pregnant woman who needed a job, and she needed an employee.

"Is that a yes?" Jewel held her breath. Since

Mason had offered her the house at cost, she could afford an employee.

Beth smiled. "Did you buy the house on Hyacinth?"

"Yes, I did. It needs a lot of work."

After a glance around the store, Beth said, "Well, you're the woman to do it."

Jewel stared at her for a moment. That statement was telling, but what did it say? Did Beth know who Jewel was, or was she simply reflecting on the work she'd already done?

"I'll have to talk to Cannon, but since they are adjusting to being parents, and he doesn't need to nap in the storeroom anymore, I'm sure he can handle it on his own."

"Okay, let me know." Jewel wrote her number on the corner of her latest list and tore it off to give to Beth. "I'll need you to start as soon as possible." They hadn't even talked about wages. "What should I pay you?"

Beth smiled. "Whatever you think is fair. I'd probably work for Fritos alone at this point."

"Fritos won't keep you independent," Jewel said.

"Nope, but they'll keep me happy."

Five minutes later, Beth walked out smiling. They agreed on a fair wage along with a supply of Fritos and Little Debbie Snacks.

The rest of the day, she worked on three lists.

One was the order in which she'd attack the re-model of her home. The second was the other property. The last was all the reasons Mason shouldn't attract her. It started with his awful taste in shoes, but as she examined it, sometime between the first entry and last, something changed. Her last entry was his amazing eyes—those blue eyes. Not blue like hers, but the color of shallow Caribbean water. She tore the list from the notebook and threw it away.

"Don't get distracted."

"Talking to yourself again?"

She spun around to see Mason leaning on the doorjamb of the back door.

"Would you stop sneaking up on me? You're going to give me a heart attack, and then who will save your ass, or should I say inheritance."

He frowned. "Fine, but maybe you shouldn't leave your back door unlocked, especially when you're focused on something else." He moved toward her, and before she could stop him, he snatched her discarded list from the trash bin.

"Give that to me."

"Nope." Shaking his head, he backed away a few steps. "Reasons Mason shouldn't attract me," he said. "Oh, this is going to be good."

She flew off the stool and tried grabbing the page, but he held it above his head and read it.

"His awful taste in shoes? Well, okay, you hate my loafers."

He continued to look at the page while she tried to nab it, hopping and jumping, but never able to reach it.

"You don't like my eyes?"

She crossed her arms and harrumphed. "Of course, I like your eyes. I just don't enjoy liking them. You're a distraction."

He crumpled the page and tossed it back into the bin, then tapped her nose with his finger. "I'm a good distraction. You'll see."

"God help me." She let her arms fall to her sides. "Is there a reason you're here?"

"I brought the contract." He looked at his watch. "It's almost closing time, and I thought I could take you to the diner for dinner, and we'll get everything in order."

It was ten to six, and her stomach was getting grumbly, but she had a Crock-Pot of chili upstairs.

"Tell you what, grab a small sour cream and a package of shredded cheddar from the cooler, and you can join me upstairs for chili."

"You're inviting me to your place?"

She tossed her head back to avoid an eye roll. "This isn't a date. It's dinner and business."

"Fine." He went to the cooler and grabbed a six-pack of Corona, the sour cream, and the cheese and came to the counter. "Ring me up. This is my contribution."

"You know I own the store, right?"

"Yes, and I also know that after tonight, you'll have a mortgage, and every penny counts."

"What would you know about pennies? That trust must be impressive for you to live in that dump while we refurb it."

He paid with a twenty. "It's substantial."

He didn't have to answer, but she kind of wanted to know. "It must be for you to lower your standards so far."

He shook his head. "Aspen Cove isn't lowering my standards. I used to come here in the summer with Wes, and I've always loved the place, and that's why I convinced the board to invest. My inner child lives here."

She rang up his items and gave him the change.

"So, you have ties to the community?"

"I have broken ties, but I still love the town."

She noticed the sadness that clouded his eyes but didn't prod for more. "What's not to love?" She bagged his purchases and moved to the door to lock it and flip the open sign to closed.

"You never met Bea Bennett, but that woman was the heartbeat of this town. Aspen Cove is like a body. Doc is the brain, Bea was the heart, Maisey the stomach, and all the other residents are the rest."

She never thought about it that way but could see his analogy. "Now Katie seems like the heartbeat, and Louise has a big enough family to keep several of the other organs functioning. If you know Peter Larkin, then you've met the town comedian. That man thinks I should marry him and have his babies."

"That old lecher is still around?"

"Yes, and still getting it on with anyone and everyone." She moved toward the staircase that led to her hovel. "I hear he may be Mrs. Brown's boy toy."

"What happened to Mr. Brown? He used to give me Tootsie Pops when I was a kid."

She heard lots of the town gossip but wasn't one to spread it, but the Brown's story was too funny not to.

She trudged up the stairs. "Supposedly, Mrs. Brown dressed her cat and her husband in matching outfits, and when he got sick, he didn't fight it. Better to die than subject himself to her fashion sense." She glanced down at Mason's shoes and smiled. He was in his boots again. "I see you're acclimating to your environment."

She flung open the door and entered her place. While it usually smelled of liniment and stale cigarettes, today, it smelled like chili. "Welcome to my humble abode."

He followed her inside and whistled. "Wow, it's amazing what a difference a good cleaning does."

"It's still a shithole, but it works."

He moved to the kitchen table. "It smells delicious. I thought I smelled something when I entered the store today but wasn't sure it wasn't something you sold."

"I try to Crock-Pot cook something weekly. It's easy, and the meals are comforting." Her phone buzzed with a message from Beth saying she could start as soon as the next day.

Jewel let out a whoop.

"Good news?" He set the bag on the table and went to the Crock-Pot to lift the lid. "Looks amazing."

"It is, and yes, the news is good. Beth is coming to work for me tomorrow so I can focus on our projects. Now grab two bowls from above the sink, and let's eat so you can sign over my house."

"Deal."

While he got the bowls, she texted Beth to tell her to meet at the store at ten the next day for her one day of baptism-by-fire training.

She and Mason enjoyed a bowl of chili and a beer. After they finished, he did the dishes, which made her want to dislike him more. Everyone around her had something negative to say about the man, but short of his poor taste in beer and foot apparel, he was a decent guy. Not her type, she kept reminding herself, but there wasn't anything about him that made her want to bathe in bleach each time she saw him.

Once he finished with the dishes, he ran down to his car to get the contracts, and half an hour later, she had signed the dotted line. It would take a day or two for the paperwork to be official, but he handed her the keys, anyway.

"When can we start?"

She smiled. "I already have. I put a list together of what we'll tackle first. While I'm training Beth tomorrow, you can gut the kitchen."

"Gut the kitchen?"

"Yes, take out your frustration about your situation on the cabinets as you demo them. By tomorrow night, when I check on you, it better be an empty box."

"Where am I supposed to eat?"

She reached over and slapped his arm. "Don't be a baby. Either eat at the diner or come to my place."

"Are you always this bossy?"

She laughed. "No, sometimes I'm worse."

# CHAPTER SEVEN

The kitchen was now the bare box Jewel had envisioned—only two days and tons of cuts and scrapes later.

"Sorry, I'm slow."

She sighed. "It's not that you're slow; you're just inexperienced."

He leaned against the wall and sipped the coffee she brought him. "Inexperience is not something associated with my name."

"No one likes a braggart." She put on her gloves and pressed the scraper under the old linoleum flooring, and it cracked into pieces with a gentle push.

"Does the floor come first?"

"No, we have electrical issues to deal with." She popped up the last of the tile and set the scraper to the side. "I've got an electrician coming in from Copper Creek soon. He'll be able to tell us what we need to do to get this up to code. The plumbing and electrical will be your biggest expenses. The rest is just jewelry."

A knock sounded at the front door. "Hello?"

Mason recognized that voice. It was the devil's. "Oh, shit."

"That must be the electrician."

He shook his head. "Nope, that's my father."

He watched her eyes widen. "Oh." She moved to the doorway and peeked out. "Should I dash out the back door?"

He chuckled. "I can see why you'd want to."

"Mason?" His father's gruff voice echoed through the home.

"In here," he said with a groan. He looked at Jewel. "I'm sorry in advance." He'd gotten to know her over the last few days, and she was unlike anyone he ever met. Within their first hour of working together, he knew she was the brains of *Reno or Wreck It*.

"What a piece of crap," his father said as he entered the kitchen. "You think you're going to redeem yourself with two properties like this?"

He stared at Mason like he was dust on his father's shoes. It shouldn't surprise him. Trenton Van der Veen would never get the father of the year award.

As if he just noticed Mason wasn't alone, he straightened his tie and turned his displeasure into a fake smile.

"Well, now, who do we have here?" His father cocked his head and grinned. "You're that woman from—"

Jewel stepped forward and offered him her hand. He wanted to warn that if she shook his father's hand, it was like making a silent deal with the devil.

"I'm Jewel."

Mason saw his father look deep into her eyes. Those eyes drew you in like a whirlpool until you were drowning in their depths.

"Hello, Jewel. It looks like my son isn't as incompetent as I once thought. Bringing you on board might help." He turned to his son. "You're getting this on film, right? We talked about this. She could bring Elite Properties publicity we couldn't buy."

While that was his original intent, having gotten to know Jewel, he wasn't ready to use her to get what he needed. The trade he made with her was fair to both of them. He wouldn't manipulate her to please his father.

"She's not your show pony."

"I'll be at my place when you want to continue," Jewel said.

"You live around here?" His father asked.

"Dad, it's none of your business."

Jewel looked at him like she was trying to solve a puzzle. "You know where to find me."

She was only halfway to the door when his father said, "You tapping that?"

"What the hell is your problem?"

He knew Jewel had heard his father, and it made his insides turn. Her history with one philandering man in her life was enough. She probably thought all men were lechers. Maybe most were, but he saw first-hand how hurt his mother was each time his dad took an interest in a new secretary or intern or masseuse. Hell, he had an affair with his proctologist, and she saw firsthand his asshole tendencies.

"My problem is that you have two houses to sell."

The best way to get rid of his father was to disappoint him. "I sold the one next door already."

His father's brows lifted. "That's my boy. How much did you make?"

It all came down to profit.

"Nothing. I gave it to her at cost."

He watched the red rise from the tip of his father's tie to the top of his bald head. It kind of reminded him of one of those cartoons where the character turned into a thermometer ready to burst.

"Haven't I taught you anything? Never let your Johnson make financial decisions."

"Considering my limited resources, I made the best decision I could. It was to sell two properties in substandard condition for less money or dump one and spend the hundred grand on refurbing the other to unload for a profit. You didn't set any prerequisites. Your directive was to sell both properties to get my trust reinstated."

"I meant for a profit."

"You'll get your profit, and I'll get my trust."

"We'll see."

Games were his father's strong point. He never played unless he could win.

"Why do you care? It's not like the trust came from you." His grandfather, Tobin Van der Veen, was the one who provided the thirty-five million.

"Because it's family money."

Mason shook his head. "Wrong, it's *my* money."

His dad stomped his handmade Italian loafer on the floor, sending up a cloud of dust.

"Wrong. It's in the trust, and I'm the trustee. You do as I say, or you get nothing."

He was so tired of asking how high when his father said jump. As soon as he got the money, he'd never do Trenton's bidding again. Real estate was who he was; it was what he did to survive.

"Be careful. You might scuff your shoes." Another glace at his dad's loafers made him cringe. They were dreadful and similar to the ones Jewel razzed him about incessantly. As soon as his father left, he was tossing them. Anything he could do to distance himself now would help him in the future.

"You've got less than sixty days."

"You're counting on me to fail."

His father laughed. "I know you will."

That should've been a sharp slice to his heart, but he'd learned long ago that his father's love wasn't something he could gain or earn. A man had to have a heart to love, and his dad's had turned to stone long before Mason was born. Maybe he'd inherited the granite organ from Tobin. Some traits were handed down from generation to generation, like eye color or male-pattern baldness. He couldn't believe that an inability to love was one of them.

Thankfully, he'd inherited his mother's conscience along with her eyes.

"Have you talked to Mom lately?"

If the subject of the homes didn't put a fire under his father's ass to leave, talking about his mother would. His parents stayed married for appearance's sake only.

In his father's own words, he once said, "It was cheaper to keep her."

That was probably true. After over thirty years of marriage, his mother would've taken half of everything, and there was no way his father was diminishing his net worth. His mother didn't care. All she wanted was to be rid of him. She'd never remarry, and maybe staying married ensured that her soft heart would never be available for the taking.

"She's in Nepal, or that's what her credit card statements say." He moved to the door, as Mason had expected. "She's spending my retirement on meditation classes."

"And you're planning on spending my trust on a masseuse with talented hands. Life is all about choices."

Trenton moved quickly through the living room furnished with a leather sofa that cost more than the kitchen remodel.

"Are you sure you don't want to stick around and lend a hand? It could be a real bonding moment for the two of us." Now he was just poking the bear.

"Get your head out of your ass and your junk back in your pants. She may be pretty, but she will not save you."

"Maybe not, but at least she offers something other than contempt."

"Son, she suckered you into a deal. Think with the head on your shoulders."

He marched in front of his father and opened the door. "I offered her the deal. She wanted nothing to do with me."

His father reached into his pocket for his keys.

"Looks like Demolition Barbie and I have something in common."

Mason closed the door and leaned against it until the rage that pumped like a spewing volcano calmed to a bubbling cauldron.

"Don't let him get to you."

"Now you're talking to yourself."

He jumped at the sound of her voice.

"Holy hell, you're like a ninja. You scared the living crap out of me."

"Is he gone?"

Feeling sad and slightly ashamed that he carried the same DNA, he let his shoulders sag forward.

"Sorry about that."

She handed him a soda and frowned. "Was I part of your plan all along?"

He didn't want to lie to her, but he also didn't want to piss her off.

"I'm not sure what you mean."

She flopped onto his sofa. "What I mean is your father made it sound like you'd pitched me as part of your plan."

He took two deep breaths. "It's not like that." With a push of his foot on the door, he propelled himself forward and walked to the couch to take a seat on the other end. "When I first saw you, the thought crossed my mind. I even pitched the idea to you, but you were dead set against it, so I dropped it."

"But your father knew I was here."

Thoughts of his father's underhandedness made him want to yank out his hair, but it was one thing he had that his dad didn't, so he was keeping it.

"He didn't know it was you. I might have mentioned something about a home renovation show, but he shut that down immediately. So, no, he didn't know you were the person I had in mind."

She chewed the inside of her cheek. "So that we're clear. No cameras. No videos. I got my life back, and I want to keep it that way. If it got out that I was up here refurbing properties, all hell would break loose. It might be good PR for Elite Properties, but it would be devastating for me. Got it."

"Got it. I won't do anything to compromise your privacy." He was as good as his word, but he couldn't control his father. All he could hope for was the usual disregard he paid him. While he hated being overlooked all these years, he wanted to remain invisible now.

"What's next?"

"The electrician will be here in a few minutes. You can clean up the tiles while I figure out what we're tackling next."

"You're the brains, and I'm the brawn."

She sipped her soda. "No." She laughed. "You're the beefcake."

# CHAPTER EIGHT

"What would you say if we took down the wall between the kitchen and the living room?" Jewel stood near the couch, looking toward the kitchen. With its single door entry, it closed off the living space from the heart of the home.

"Are you sure you want to mess with walls these days?"

If she weren't afraid of ruining his cream-colored leather sofa, she would have lobbed her coffee at him for even bringing up the *Reno or Wreck It* debacle. Still, she liked her coffee strong enough to put hair on a man's chest and dark enough to stain the sofa color black, so it was sure to ruin the leather if it spilled.

"I told you it wasn't my fault."

"Yes, you did." He gripped both sides of the

doorway and leaned in and out of it the way a kid did when he was debating between leaving to play video games with his friends or staying for one more warm brownie. "Do you think it will bring value to the house?"

It was a stupid question, and by the grin on his face, he knew it. "Is it always about the money with the Van der Veens?"

He stopped moving as if she'd punched him in the gut, but he sucked in a breath and seemed to recover.

"No, it's not always about the money, but in this case, it is. Most of our budget is going into the kitchen and the bathrooms."

"As it should," she countered. A house with a lousy kitchen would never sell. Going cheap on the bathrooms was a kiss of death.

"All I'm asking is, for a town as small as Aspen Cove, do you think the high-end structural changes are necessary?"

She gripped her Styrofoam cup and judged the distance. "Can you step back about a foot or so?"

He did without asking why. The man sure had a lot of questions about everything else, but he didn't question her current request, and as soon as he was safely in the kitchen, she flung her to-go cup from the diner his way; it floated as if in slow motion and hit its target smack dab in the middle of his chest.

Since it was her morning coffee, it was close to room temp.

"What the hell?" He stared down at his T-shirt and watched as the dark chocolate color bled into the red material.

"Are you seriously asking me if it's worth it? You're an agent, and if you're a good one, you know the answer to that question." She moved toward him.

"Fine, can we afford to tear down the wall?"

He peeled off his wet shirt, which stopped her dead in her tracks. Who knew all that man muscle was hiding under the cotton?

She stared at him for several seconds, or maybe it was minutes, she wasn't sure. All she knew was Mason looked good in her coffee.

"Go put some clothes on. You're distracting me."

He chuckled. "I seem to do that a lot, lately." Making no move toward his room, he stood there shirtless and as appetizing as a container of red licorice. "You didn't answer the question."

She shook her head, trying to clear her thoughts. "There was a question?"

Moving forward, he was now so close she could smell the coffee on him. "Shall we get this out of the way?"

She tilted her chin to look up at him. "Get what out of the way?"

"This." His hand wrapped around the back of

her neck, and his finger threaded through her short hair. With a gentle tug, he pulled her to him until their lips met.

The kiss was hesitant at first but grew with intensity the longer their lips stayed fused. When she opened her mouth to suck in extra air, his tongue delved inside and danced with hers. He tasted like all the good things in life: fine wine, Belgium chocolate, a perfect wine reduction.

Her hands rested against his now dry chest, fingers skimming across the smattering of hair and exploring the hills and valleys of hours spent in the gym.

With another tug, he pulled away but left his fingers twined in her hair.

"Wow," he said. "That was..."

Gaining a moment of clarity, she stepped back, forcing him to drop his grip on her. "Totally wrong." Her lips still tasted the rightness of the kiss, but her brain screamed something that sounded like, are you nuts? But she was because all she wanted to do was step forward and get lost in his lips again.

She spun around to stop herself from acting impulsively.

"Yes, we can afford to tear down the wall. I don't think it's load-bearing, but we should get a structural engineer to make sure I'm not wrong. I think at this point in my life, checks and balances would go a long way."

"You don't have to hide from me, Jewel." He moved behind her, setting his hands on her shoulders and turning her to face him. "You know as well as I do that kiss was going to happen."

She reached up and touched her lips. "It shouldn't have."

He leaned down and pressed his forehead to hers. "But it did, and it will again. That was too good not to indulge."

"Go get dressed."

"I like the way you stare at me."

Feeling flustered, she picked up the sledge-hammer and whacked the drywall a few times.

"I'm not staring at you."

"You are."

"Am not." The last time she had a conversation like this, she was in elementary school.

"Are too, but since we're behind schedule, I'll do as you say and get a shirt on. Try not to spill your coffee on me again."

She laughed. He was right; they'd been dancing around each other for days. A kind of verbal foreplay destined to end in a kiss, but that was where it needed to stop.

"You know, if you didn't have to live here, we could pick up the pace, but working around your ridiculous white furniture makes it more challenging."

"It's latte, not white, and it's not ridiculous. I've seen you sit on it, and it feels good hugging your body, right?"

Other things hugged her body better than his soft calfskin, but she didn't have time to relive the kiss and the way he seemed to wrap himself around her.

"It's comfortable, I'll give you that, but if the house were empty, we could plow right through things."

"Where am I supposed to live?"

She pointed toward her newly purchased house. "You can stay at my place."

He lifted a brow and the corner of his lip while giving her an adorable look.

"Are you inviting me to live with you, Jewel?"

She grunted something unladylike and rolled her eyes. "No, I'm telling you to move your shit temporarily next door."

"Are you sure that's what you mean?" He closed the inches between them again. "I'm pretty certain you meant I could live with you."

She put her hand on his chest and pinched several hairs between her fingers before she twisted, causing him to yelp and step back.

"Nope, I'm fairly certain I meant you could stay there temporarily while we fix your life."

He rubbed at the space where she'd plucked several hairs from his chest.

"I thought the breaker was shot."

She smiled and stepped away. "I fixed it."

"When?"

She let out an exasperated breath. "When we quit here, I go over there. I've been working by lantern light, but I replaced the faulty breakers, and it's all good." She looked at her phone and frowned. "Listen, I have to go. Beth needs to get off early today for a doctor's appointment. I bet you could get some volunteers to move your stuff to my place. Just the big stuff. We can work around the little things."

She walked to the door. "And make sure you get that drywall down. We'll need to find someone to confirm what I already know."

"I've got a guy."

"I used to."

"I'm on it." He pulled his phone from his pocket. "And Jewel?"

"What?" She tried to sound annoyed, but there was that hint of playful sexiness in her voice.

"You know you want to kiss me again."

Looking over her shoulder at him and moving out the door, she said, "Oh yeah, I want that as much as I want a nail in my shoe."

"I never pegged you as a masochist."

"No? I stayed married for four years. I'd say I'm well versed in pain and torture."

"Maybe you should change your name?"

"I can't. Monroe was my maiden name too. Although, we don't share DNA."

"No, I meant instead of Jewel, we call you Jade as in you're jaded. Not every guy is an asshole."

He walked into the brisk air, and she watched the goosebumps rise on his skin.

"Are you saying you're not?"

He crossed his arms over his chest. "Oh, I can be an asshole, but I'm not the kind that would ruin your reputation and take away your dreams."

She stopped at the front of her house. "No? What kind of asshole are you then?"

"I'm the asshole who won't take no for an answer. You feel this thing building between us. It's going somewhere."

She opened the door to her house and reached for the jacket and keys she'd hung there earlier. "It's going nowhere." She nodded toward his place. "I'd suggest you get moving. You've got a lot to do."

She removed the house key from her ring. "Lock it up when you're not here."

Two steps away from her Porsche, she heard him say, "You're wrong."

She climbed into her car and backed out of the driveway. God, she hoped *he* was wrong, but the way her body tingled each time he was near, she knew he was right.

When she got to the store and relieved Beth, she started another list called *Ways to discourage Mason*.

At the top, she wrote, *Drop something else on his head.*

# CHAPTER NINE

Jewel was always leaving him lists of things to do. Then again, lists seemed to be her thing.

He parked his car in front of the Bishop's Bait and Tackle Shop. With the lake at a hard freeze this time of year, Bowie did a good deal of business with the hardcore anglers who would cut a hole in the ice and drop in a line rather than wait for late spring to start sportfishing again.

When he got out of his SUV, the smell of freshly baked blueberry muffins wafted through the air, and it reminded him of a bearhug from Heidi. Although she'd always stick one raspberry in the batch, and whoever got it was given a second muffin. Somehow Mason always got that muffin, and he was sure it was her way of telling him he was special.

The sweetness pulled him from his original destination and drew him right inside the bakery.

"Hey, you need something to sweeten your disposition." There was a twang to Katie's voice that always made him smile. If that didn't do it, her LED smile would.

"My disposition is just fine, but I could use a coffee and a muffin to keep me sweet." The last coffee he had that morning never touched his lips but his chest.

"I hear you're staying in town with us for a bit." Katie lifted a bag and a plate as if asking if he wanted a to-go order. He pointed to the bag because he had a lot of stuff to accomplish to get an A on his daily report card.

"It's a long story, but the short answer is yes. That's why I'm here. I was going to ask your husband for a hand moving some big stuff from my house to Jewel's, but you lured me into the bakery rather than the bait shop."

"Funny, nice play on words." She popped a K-cup into the coffeemaker and pressed the button. Mixed with the smell of sugar and spices came the strong brew. Next to being bossed around by Jewel, this was his second favorite place in town unless it was fried chicken night at the diner. Maisey's chicken would take the lead any day.

"Have a seat, and I'll round up a crew for you."

She pointed to the chair by the window, then handed him his to-go bag. Grabbing her phone, she dialed.

"Hey, baby," she purred into the phone. "I need you ... right now."

She hung up and giggled. "That should get him over here mighty fast."

Mason shook his head. "Do they teach that in school?"

"In Texas, they do." Her shoulders shook with laughter. "It's called etiquette 102. The 101 class is all about manners. The follow-on is about getting what you want when you want it."

Mason reached into the bag and pulled the muffin top loose. Though he wasn't into Katie, it was fascinating watching a woman at work.

"Guys are the inferior creature." He took a bite and hummed.

"That you're willing to admit it means you're slightly evolved."

"Don't give me too much credit; I'm still a man."

"True," she said and smiled. "Looks like your help has arrived."

The door opened, and in walked Bowie. He saw Mason and frowned. "What's up, love? You said you *needed* me."

Bowie emphasized the word needed.

"I do, baby." She rocked her head from shoulder

to shoulder, then nodded toward Mason. "I needed you to help him."

"I thought ..." Bowie grumbled.

"I know what you thought, and I'll reward you for your efforts."

Bowie laughed. "Dude, be careful. Women are like spiders. They attract you with their webs, and once you're trapped, you'll do anything for their bite."

"Oh, he knows," Katie said. "He's moving in with Jewel."

Bowie's brows shot north. "You and Jewel?"

While the thought warmed his insides a little, he had to nip that one in the bud right away. "Oh, no. I sold her a house, and she agreed to let me store my stuff there until I'm finished refurbing my home." It was sort of the truth. Even though she demanded he move his furniture, the result was the same.

Katie leaned in like she was telling a secret. "You know who she is, right?"

His heart fell to his gut. "Umm." He didn't want to admit anything. Somehow, whatever he said right then seemed like it would be wrong. If he admitted to knowing, he'd seem like the slimy guy they all thought he was. If he played stupid, he was an idiot.

Katie handed Bowie a cup of coffee and a cookie like it was a reward for coming when called.

"Look," she said. "We all know who she is, but if

she wants to pretend that we don't, the town is happy to play along. Surely she's heard the whispers. She can color her hair and wear contacts for all I care, but she isn't fooling anyone. JJ Monroe has a presence, and when she walks into a room, you know it."

He wanted to laugh because that was true. Even if Jewel didn't have such mesmerizing eyes, all a person had to do was look at her, and they'd recognize her confidence. Maybe that was why he liked her. She didn't need to bullshit her way through life. She had a specific set of skills uncommon for a woman, and those set her apart from the rest.

"Very true."

"Let me call Cannon. He's the muscle in our mix. I'm the brains," Bowie stated.

Katie moved around the corner and sidled up next to her husband. "Oh no, baby. You're everything." She lifted on tiptoes and pecked Bowie's lips. "Your mom is babysitting tonight." She stared at him. "I'll be home by five. Don't be late."

Bowie pulled his phone to his ear. "Bro, get your butt to the house on Hyacinth. Mason needs a hand with a few things." He hung up before his brother had time to respond. "Let's go. It would appear I've got a hot date tonight."

Mason pulled out a ten to pay, but Katie shook her head. "It's on me. Usually, I give the first muffin away for free."

Bowie laughed. "Be careful, man. She's like a crack dealer. She gives you the first hit for free, and then you're hooked." He kissed her and walked to the door. "See you tonight, baby."

Mason followed Bowie outside. "How does that feel?"

Bowie stopped and faced him. "What?"

"Knowing you found the one."

Bowie smiled. "There's a perfect heart for everyone. I was lucky enough to find mine twice."

Mason knew there was a special meaning to his words. He'd heard the rumors but wasn't sure they were true. Now he was.

"Your story is Hallmark worthy."

"Nah, my story is simply about love, except that mine has two women with the same heart. I'll meet you there." He ran into the bait shop, and Mason left in his car.

By the time he got to the house, Cannon was already there.

"Hey man, what's up?"

"Need to shift some stuff from this house to that one."

Cannon looked from one house to another. "Isn't that one Jewel's? I heard she bought it." He grinned. "Can't wait to see what she does with the place. Took her long enough to work on The Corner Store."

It's funny how everyone in town knew exactly

who she was, but no one made a big deal of it. "I think she's flexing her muscles now. It takes some time to get used to a new norm."

He moved toward the door of the house he occupied.

"Don't I know it. I helped make a human. I look at Michael each day and can't believe something so amazing came about because I loved his mom." Cannon followed Mason into the house. "Are you and Jewel ... a thing?"

That kiss told him they could be. There was no denying the chemistry, but he would deny the connection. "No, we're..." What were they? He'd like to say friends but wasn't sure she would agree. "Partnering in getting this house ready to sell."

"Make sure you treat her right. We take care of ours here in town, and she's one of ours."

"Why does everyone think I'm such a bad guy?" He moved to the end of the sofa. "Let's start with this."

As they lifted it, Bowie walked inside the house. "Is the door unlocked?" He nodded toward Jewel's place.

"It is, but don't tell Jewel. She's still convinced someone will break in and steal what she doesn't have in there."

Bowie moved ahead of them to the front door and

opened it wide. "If they do, it'll be your shit they're stealing."

"Mason was asking why everyone thought he was a bad guy," Cannon said as he lowered the sofa to the floor.

"Hmm, you want a list?" Bowie asked.

The words he told Jewel floated in his head about not letting someone else define you, but he was interested in hearing the reputation he'd built in the few interactions he'd had. "Bullet points would be fine."

"No roof in Baxter's place," Bowie said.

"Hole in the floor in a place you showed Mercy," Cannon added.

The brothers volleyed back and forth until they said, "Rodents," at the same time.

Mason raised his hands. "Hey, I don't create the messes. I just sell them. A house is only worth what a buyer will pay for it." Those were also the words he told Jewel.

"Hard to negotiate a fair deal when there are limited resources available."

"Supply and demand," Mason countered.

"Just don't mess with her. She's a nice person," Cannon said.

"Have you listened to her? She's got a razor blade for a tongue. That woman can shred you to pieces with a sentence."

"Glad to hear she can hold her own." Bowie

looked around. "She'll whip this place into shape in no time."

They went back to the house next door.

"She's the reason you guys are here. She says jump, and I ask how high?"

The brothers looked at each other and burst out laughing.

"Sounds like love to me," Bowie said.

Mason picked up an end table on his own. "Nope, this is purely business."

"Right," Cannon grabbed one end of the coffee table while Bowie picked up the other. "That's what I told myself too. Sage was a pain in my ass, but I always found an excuse for why I needed her around me."

He led the way out the door. "Seriously, this is purely a business relationship."

"You kiss her yet," Bowie asked.

Mason didn't endorse or deny it, and that confirmed it. "Shall we get the rest?"

"Nice change of subject." They went back to the house to grab another load. "Which means yes, and that means you're lying to yourself." Bowie shrugged. "We all do it, and then we realize the truth. There are certain women men can't live without." He held up a finger. "One's a good barber. I like the women better because they always rub your neck and pay closer attention to details." The second finger popped up. "Can't live without your mom." A third finger rose. "And the woman who stole your heart."

"You guys are like maples that sprung a leak." Mason let out the sound a person made when they tasted something foul. "So sappy."

"You tease now, but by the time this house is finished, you two will stand at the end of my dock, exchanging vows," Bowie said.

He almost dropped the lamp he was hauling. "That will never happen."

They worked for the next two hours, shifting furniture from place to place. Thankfully, Mason was a minimalist. He loved high-quality Danish furnishings but not a lot of knick-knacks.

Once he was alone, he called the structural engineer that Elite often used, set up an appointment, and then went to work on removing the drywall. He knew Jewel was doing her due diligence by getting a professional to confirm what she already realized—this wasn't a load-bearing wall. If she thought there was the slightest chance, she wouldn't have had him demo it.

"Hello," her voice echoed through the empty living room. "Holy hell, you got it all done." She walked toward him, carrying a brown sack and a drink tray.

"You gave me a list of things to do."

She scoffed. "Yeah, but I didn't expect you to do them."

"Then why tell me what you want done?"

"It was a test."

He walked over and took the bag from her. "I'm an excellent student." He opened it and inhaled. "Did you bring me a bacon cheeseburger?"

She snatched the bag back. "Yes, but it's not a reward. It's fuel because we're pulling an all-nighter." She spun around and trotted toward the door. "Let's use that fine teak table sitting in the dining room of my house. It's the only time you'll be able to rest tonight."

He made like he was wielding a whip and mimicked the cracking sound. "Do you ever let up?"

She stopped and looked over her shoulder. "Last time I did, my entire world imploded."

He watched as the bright blue rim of her irises turned a cloudy gray and made a silent promise to try to not disappoint this woman.

As they continued their journey, he said, "I called the structural engineer, and he'll be out tomorrow."

"Are you sure you're a trust fund baby? I mean, you're not as useless as I expected you to be."

"Is that supposed to wound?"

They entered her house and went straight to the dining room. He had to admit; his furniture looked good there. Or maybe she looked good with his furniture. His life was becoming such a blur.

"No, it's a compliment."

"Delivered with your unique warmth."

She held out her hand. "Welcome to the team, Mason. Let me introduce myself. I'm Jade."

He loved the way she threw his words back at him and how she gave as good as she got. But what he loved most was that she felt comfortable enough to be herself. If he wasn't so preoccupied with other things, he could probably give loving Jewel Monroe a try. Not forever love, but the kind that dirtied his Egyptian cotton sheets.

"What are you smiling at?" She asked.

He hadn't realized he was. "You don't want to know."

"Eat up; we've got a lot to do."

"You have another list for me?" He bit into his burger and felt the juice run down his chin.

"Yes," she grinned. "Stop being a pig."

"You sure you don't want to add something about my shoes."

"You already know how I feel about those shoes."

"I do, which is why I tossed them."

"You did not." She said with a level of shock mixed with awe.

"I did." He'd chucked them right after his father left. He wanted to be many things, but resembling his father was not one of them, and seeing him wear the same shoes sealed the deal. Anything Trenton Van der Veen had needed to go, including the driving shoes.

"Why?"

"Because you hated them."

"Why do you care what I think?"

He dipped a fry in ketchup and popped it into his mouth. "I don't know why, but I do." That was the question of the day. Why did he? "Don't get any funny ideas of us getting married on the end of Bowie's dock. That isn't ever going to happen."

Her head snapped back like he'd slapped her. "As if. In your wildest dreams. You're not my type."

"What's your type."

"I like a man who's... absent."

"Then we're a perfect match because as soon as we finish this house, I'm out of here." He popped another fry into his mouth and spoke around it. "What's next?"

He watched her soften and then spring to life as she pulled a list from her jeans pocket and went over exactly what they'd accomplish that night. She was firmly in her element. How in the hell did the show survive without her?

# CHAPTER TEN

It was an abnormally frigid morning when Jewel got up and saw her breath. She hoped Mason had turned up the heat at both houses. They had developed a routine where she would show up at the home she bought and have coffee and whatever Mason had for breakfast. At first, it was a bowl of cereal, but lately, he'd upped his game. Yesterday it was some kind of scramble. The day before that, it was oatmeal and bacon.

In hindsight, she should've given him the studio above the store, but since his furniture had to be moved, it made sense to shift him like one of his lamps, straight across the driveway.

"Why the hell is it so damn cold in here?" Every exhale came out as a white cloud. She raced to the old thermostat and saw it was thirty-two degrees and a shiver ran through her. "Shit."

There was no need to use the lights in the morning because of her east-facing windows, but when she flipped the switch and got nothing, she groaned.

"Bad timing for a power outage."

She had so much to do today. If the power was out all over town, she couldn't lay the new flooring in Mason's house. This entire day was going to hell in a handbasket mighty fast. That was one of her father's favorite sayings. That, and colder than a witch's tit. She always wondered how cold that was and concluded it was precisely the temperature of her hovel above the store.

After texting Beth and telling her not to come in, Jewel walked out the front of her building and noticed that only her side of the street had no power. The bakery's lights were on, as were the bait shop and the sheriff's office. The scent of fresh baked goods floated in the breeze.

"Just my luck." She climbed into her SUV and drove to Hyacinth. Seeing the lights on in her new home appeared her luck might not be so bad after all. At least Mason wouldn't leave her in the dark.

Earlier that week, the engineer confirmed what she already knew. The wall wasn't load-bearing, and the house had a roomier wide-open feel with the barrier gone, but that wasn't the true reason she wanted the wall to come down. She was suffering from a lack of confidence. Being blamed for the mishap shook her self-assurance. She'd never questioned her decisions before that day, and it turned out she should've been questioning everything all along.

"Hey," she said when she walked in the door.

Mason peeked his head around the corner. "Come on in. I made French toast."

She smiled like a lunatic. Mason had her at the scramble, but she was a goner anytime fried bread, butter, and syrup were on the menu. The way to her heart was through simple carbohydrates.

"Are you serious? Keep cooking like this, and I'll have you on the end of Bowie's pier."

"You'd have to hogtie me. You've been married, so you know … it's not a good gig. I've watched my parents serve their sentences for over thirty years. I would've thought they would've paroled themselves by now, but it's cheaper to keep her."

She laughed. "Mine was much shorter. I got let loose at four years."

He set a plate on the table and served her a coffee.

"Was it good at the beginning?" he asked.

She cut a bite-sized morsel and stuck it in her mouth, savoring the texture, the creaminess of the butter, and the sweetness of the maple syrup. She tasted the quality of the ingredients—only the best for Mr. Van der Veen.

"We met on the set. It was kind of like the bachelor wears a tool belt."

"Oh, wow. I didn't start watching until the second season. You met and fell in love and got married?"

She rocked her head from side to side. She wished it had been that romantic, but it was kind of a sad story in hindsight. "Kind of."

"How do you kind of get married?"

"Oh no, we did that. It's the fell in love part." She cut another bite and swirled it in the syrup. "We were together twenty-four seven. Now that I've had time to think about it, getting married was more for the show than it was for us."

"The show pressured you?"

She wouldn't call it pressure, but they certainly made it nearly impossible not to. They were so busy there was no way to have a relationship with anyone else.

"It was just a puzzle that went together smoothly, but in the end, when we looked at it, it was missing several pieces. You can't finish a masterpiece if the key ingredients aren't there." It was the first time she'd ever voiced that opinion, and it freed her. "Marrying Matt was like saying I do to a friend. I'd always heard you should marry your best friend. I just didn't think he'd start sleeping with mine."

"What?" He dug into his French toast like it was a battle of wills, and he was determined to win. He severed a piece and crammed it into his mouth.

She took a few more bites while she considered her situation. All in all, they had a good run. She was grateful no children came from their union. Waiting was part of the plan. Maybe they both knew from the beginning that it would never work out.

"Yes, it's a twisted tale, but things happen for a reason, right?" She pointed her empty fork at him. "Look at you needing me, and me needing this house, and then you needing this house so we could fix yours. That's also very twisted, but it seems right."

"It does but your best friend?"

"Everyone has an agenda." She waved his question away with a sweep of her hand. "Yours is getting this house ready to sell." She took a sip of coffee. "The deal gets sweeter every day I show up, and you have breakfast and brew ready. Do you know how to make cheese blintzes?"

He held up his phone. "No, but I've got Google."

"You're too good to me."

He smiled. "And you were too good for him. Are you sure you don't want to record this and set the record straight? It doesn't have to be a big deal, but if you blogged about it, you could prove to everyone who ran the show."

"The producer ran the show."

"Your friend?"

"Yes, and money talks."

He nodded. "Absolutely, and that's why I want mine."

She stood and put her plate in the sink. "Times wasting. Shall we?" She led them to the house next door. "It's downright cold." She looked over her shoulder. "Did you know that the power is out on my side of the street downtown?"

"No. That's odd."

She shrugged. "The town is old, and so is the wiring. At least it's over freezing so that the pipes won't burst."

"I hear we're in for sub-zero tonight."

"Shh, don't say that. So far, luck has been on my side. I don't want to test her."

"Luck is a female?"

Jewel smiled. "Today she is. Ask me tomorrow, and I might have a different answer."

"Oh, I see how this goes. Luck is a woman when it's good and a man when it's shit."

"You're a wise one."

She opened several boxes of flooring material and started in the kitchen. A couple of hours later, they were midway through the living room when she turned to find Mason's father behind them. He swiftly shoved his phone inside his pocket.

"I knocked," he said.

That could've been true, but she doubted it. There was a slimy Van der Veen in her presence, but it wasn't Mason. Just being in the same room with his father made her want to shower.

"What are you doing here?" Mason asked. The deep cut lines on his face showed his displeasure.

"I was in the neighborhood." He moved forward, tapping his foot on the hardwood flooring they'd just put in.

"I find that hard to believe. Shouldn't you be in the Maldives with the masseuse spending my trust fund?"

Trenton let out a villain-worthy laugh. A kind of mwah ha ha ha ha that made her skin crawl.

"That's next week. This week I'm checking in on my investment."

Jewel continued to work while father and son sparred. Peeking up, she watched Mason fist and release several times. "My investment, you mean. You gave me two properties, and what I do with them determines my future. Or did that change too? I can't figure you out. You're always changing the rules."

"You sound like your mom."

"Good. Did you need something?"

Trenton tapped his pocket and shook his head. "Got everything I need."

That's when she knew he'd taken pictures or video.

She wanted to spring to her feet and demand his phone, but he spun on his worthless loafers and walked out the door.

"Looking better than I would've thought,"—he called back— "considering we have Wreck-It Rita and Misfit Mason leading the way." He climbed into his car.

Hearing him call her that awful nickname made her sprint toward him with a hammer in her hand, but before she got there, Mason grabbed her and tugged her back.

"He's not worth it."

She sagged against him. "That was mean."

He chuckled. "You think? That was his sweet side."

She took a few calming breaths. "I'd hate to meet him on a bad day."

"You ever see an angry hornet?" He led her back to the house.

"A few have chased me."

"They're relentless. They don't quit until they've caused you pain and drove you away. That's my father."

She set her hand on his shoulder and squeezed.

"I'm sorry. I can't even imagine being raised in a hornet's nest. My parents were straight out of *Leave it to Beaver*."

"Warm cookies after school?"

"Yep," she said with a nod. "She removed the crust from the sandwich and added a little note that said *I love you* in my lunch bag each day."

"I got lunch money. If there was a note, it instilled fear."

They went back to work like a well-oiled machine, with him placing boards and her operating the nail gun.

"Did you ever get a note?"

"Oh, yes." He let out a whistle. "They were a buy one, get one. You get a letter, and he threw in an ass beating for free."

He tucked the last board in the corner, and she nailed it in place. "What were your crimes?"

He leaned against the wall. "Bad grades. Forgot a chore. Mouthed off. Stuff like that. Nothing big."

"He's not a nice man." She rose to her feet and wiped her hands on her jeans. "I think he took video or pictures of us. My gut tells me he's up to no good."

Mason lifted his hands into the air. "I wouldn't worry about it. What would he do with pictures?"

She couldn't say. "I don't know, but it makes me uncomfortable. Don't forget that I'm hiding here."

Mason laughed. "If you think you're hiding,

you're crazy. Everyone in this town knows who you are."

"No, they don't." That simply wasn't true. Only a few people recognized her. One was Goldie, and the other was Mason. The only reason Trenton knew her was because his son mentioned her while negotiating his future. Surely if someone in town realized who she was, they would've said something.

Keeping her identity under wraps was an essential component of keeping her sanity.

"Believe what you want, but it's true." His stomach let out a rumble that echoed through the empty room. "You hungry? I think it's fried chicken night at the diner."

"You buying?"

He moved to the door. "I've fed you all week. Why stop now?"

"Exactly," she said with a hint of playfulness in her voice. "I want pie too. I'm not a cheap date."

"Or easy," he said.

# CHAPTER ELEVEN

Maisey's Diner always smelled like home. Not his home, but the feeling of home when Heidi took him to her house on the occasional weekend when his father couldn't be bothered to make other arrangements.

"I love that smell," he said as they made their way to a booth in the corner.

She lifted her pert little nose into the air. "You mean the scent of cardiac arrest and high cholesterol?" She giggled. "I love it too."

"Hey, kids." Maisey stood next to the booth, swinging a pot of coffee. The hot liquid sloshed back and forth, but a drop never spilled. "You want coffee, tea, or me?"

She was always happy. It seemed to be the way of

the people in town. They embraced everything from the birth of a child to the first crocus that pushed through the frozen soil. He wasn't used to looking at the smaller things to celebrate. His upbringing was all about significant accomplishments—straight A's, million-dollar deals, and corporate takeovers.

"Not sure Ben wants to share you," Mason said, "I'll settle for iced tea."

"Same," Jewel said. "And the blue plate special." She rubbed her chin. "When did the power come back on?"

Maisey laughed. "It didn't. We have a generator. Most everyone does."

"I don't," Jewel said.

"I think you'll be all right. Your pipes share a wall and bursting hasn't happened for a few years." Maisey glanced back at him. "You blue plating it too?"

"As long as it's fried chicken, then yes."

"You got it." Maisey walked away, but the scent of her gardenia perfume lingered.

"If the power has been out all day, then your place is going to be frigid." He stared out the window at the darkening sky. A few flakes were falling.

"I'll be okay. I'm made of tough stuff." She whispered it and with little power behind her words.

"You are," he confirmed. "You'd have to be to do what you do and deal with what you did."

Maisey dropped off the iced tea and disappeared. As he looked around the room, he noticed it was empty.

"Where is everyone?" he asked.

"Hibernating?" She turned to the window, and in just those few moments, it went from flurries to an all-out snowstorm. "Holy hell, where did that come from?"

"Snow gods," Maisey said as she slid two plates of sizzling fried chicken onto the table. "I'm closing early, so if you want dessert, let me know now. I want to get home before I have to sleep on the cot in the back. Ben's a cot hog."

"Jewel wants pie."

Jewel shook her head. "No, I think I'll be okay."

"Suit yourself, but I have to tell ya, I make the best cherry pie in the state." She slid the bill onto the table and turned to walk away.

Mason saw the war happening inside Jewel. Her eyes flashed to the pie cabinet and then the snow and back to the cabinet.

He pulled out his wallet and grabbed his credit card. "Hey, Maisey, we'll take two pieces to go, and I'm ready to settle my bill."

"You didn't have to buy me pie."

He picked up a drumstick. "It was part of the bargain." He took a deep breath and thought about Jewel's description. And she was right. It smelled like cardiac arrest and high cholesterol. Anything deep-fried couldn't be good for his body, but it was good for his soul.

He bit into the crunchy outer coating and hummed. "Heaven."

Jewel dug into her mashed potatoes first and made a similar sound of satisfaction, but hers took on a sexy groan that made his body come alive.

"She doesn't know who I am. Maisey looks at me like I'm just another customer." She chomped into her drumstick, and the juice ran down her chin.

Both reached for their napkins, but she got to hers before he could lean over and wipe off her chin. There was something vulnerable about her at times like this. She looked at him with embarrassment but seemed to steel herself.

"What? It's juicy."

He raised his hands in surrender. "I didn't say a word."

She laughed. "No, but for a second, it looked like you may hop over the table and lick it off my face."

That thought hadn't crossed his mind, but it was appealing. After working side by side with her for several weeks, he experienced many things, like her laughter when something struck her as funny, her kindness when she brought him Raspberry Zingers, her fear when she turned and saw his father there.

He lied to her when he told her that his father

wasn't up to anything. He knew better. Trenton Van der Veen was a corporate card shark, and this was a game to him. If he had a card up his sleeve, he was going to play it. The problem was, Mason couldn't figure the game out.

"Where'd you go?" Jewel asked.

He shook the thoughts of his father from his head. "Just thinking about licking the juice off your face."

Her cheeks bloomed as red as the fake rose that sat in an empty vase on the table.

"You were not."

"Was so."

"Lose that thought because I've given up on men."

He sipped his tea. "Hey, just this morning, you told me you'd get me to the end of Bowie's pier for a shotgun wedding."

She huffed. "That's because you made me French toast."

He finished his last bite of mashed potatoes and pushed his nearly empty plate away.

"See, you are easy."

She picked up a spoonful of mashed potatoes and flung them at him, hitting him in the forehead before plopping onto the table.

"Did you just—"

"I saw it," Maisey said.

"Do not retaliate, or you'll both be deep cleaning the diner tonight while I watch *Wheel of Fortune*." She placed the pie boxes on the table and handed him back his credit card and the slip to sign. "You kids take your foreplay somewhere else."

"Oh," Jewel shook her head hard enough to rattle the insides. "This isn't foreplay. It's... It's... I don't know what it is, but it's not that."

Maisey tapped her pen on the bench back. "Oh, honey, I know sizzle when I see it, and what you have didn't come from the chicken." She leaned forward and picked up their plates. "Now you two get before you get stuck here all night."

"It'll never happen. I live in this building."

"Probably not tonight. I'm sure it's too cold to stay in your place, so you might have to stay in your other place." Her smile was that knowing kind, like it was already a done deal. "You're staying there, right?"

"He is, but it's not like that. We're partnering on a project."

Maisey lifted her head. "I've got eyes. I see what's happening. Maybe you should open yours." She turned to leave but stopped after a step. "You know, Mason. I didn't like you at first. I had you pegged all wrong. I listened to the chatter, and you're not a slimeball but a decent guy. Stay on this path, and I think you can redeem yourself."

That familiar itch ran up his spine. It was like a rash that took over and irritated until he wanted to crawl out of his skin—Van der Veen skin.

"A smart woman once told me never to let anyone tell you who you are."

"Your mother?" Maisey asked.

"No, my mother had few words of wisdom to offer. It was the housekeeper. She may have cleaned our home and cooked our meals, but she was a queen —queen of my heart."

Thoughts of Heidi always brought feelings of warmth and happiness, but along with those came sadness because she was no longer here.

"You're a romantic at heart. Now get your soft heart out of my diner."

He picked up the pie and waited for Jewel to put her coat on and head to the door.

"Looks like we've been dismissed."

"Would seem so," Jewel said, looking over her shoulder as the lights in the diner went out. She reached for her container of pie, but he pulled it back. "Hey, you said one of those is mine."

"You can have them both, but only after I see you home."

She narrowed her eyes, which made the crinkles in the corners more prominent. Many men liked the plumped-up Botox look, but he loved how her face changed with her emotions.

"This wasn't a date, and at thirtysomething ... I don't need you to walk me to my door."

"I didn't get a lot of pleasant lessons from my father, but walking a woman to her door was one. Humor me."

They proceeded to the end of the block where The Corner Store sat so aptly named. She entered through the front door and climbed the stairway by her phone's flashlight to her studio.

"Okay, I'm here so that you can go."

"Nope."

With a grunt of frustration, she swung the door open and froze. The light of her phone reflected off the lake of water.

"No, no, no, no, nooo," she buried her face in her hands. "I had a feeling." The first step inside came with a splash followed by the rapid *plunk splash plunk splash* of her shoes as she raced through the water to the kitchen to shut off the valve.

Thankfully, the place was small, and it didn't appear the leak had sprung long ago, or the store below would've flooded.

"What a mess." She moved to her bed and collapsed on it. What started as a whimper turned into a full-blown cry.

He sat beside her and rubbed her back. He had little experience with nurturing, but he hoped his touch helped. She moved closer to him and buried her head in his lap. "Why does my life have to be so shitty?"

He wanted to laugh. When comparing apples to oranges, neither of their lives were shitty. "Hey, shitty is when you don't have food to eat and money to keep the lights on." He pointed to the water on the floor. "This is an inconvenience."

"No, it's just one more setback. I always seem to be one step forward and two back."

"Tell you what. You gather a bag of whatever you need, and I'll start on the cleanup. We'll head to the house where I'll make you my special hot cocoa, and we can watch anything you want."

She took in a shaky breath. "You make special hot cocoa?"

He nodded. It was only special because he had some on hand, but it was instant, and maybe a sprinkle of cocoa on top would doctor it up.

He went to work, sopping up the water and squeezing it into the sink.

"I can probably fix this." She leaned down to look at the pipes.

"Not tonight, your power is out, and it's not getting warmer in here. Let me finish this, and I'll take you home." He knew in his heart it was where she belonged.

Her head hung as she nodded. "I'll sleep on the couch."

"It's your house. You'll sleep in the bed."

"It's your bed."

She had a point. "How about we both sleep in the bed? I'll stay to my side if you stay to yours."

"Are you sure you can control yourself?"

The answer was no. He liked her—everything about her.

He raised three fingers. "Scout's honor." He'd never been a Scout.

# CHAPTER TWELVE

She didn't know what the hell she was doing, but staying at her house with Mason was the only option she had.

Everything about the hard freeze was an inconvenience. Not only was her apartment a mess, but who knew what would happen to the refrigerated sections of the store.

Who was she kidding? The whole place, including her apartment, was near freezing. There was a higher risk that everything would turn to ice rather than thaw and spoil.

She pulled into her driveway and parked.

"I appreciate you letting me crash here tonight," she said as she passed him exiting his SUV.

"It's your house. I'm the thankful one. Extremely

so since you fixed the breaker box and we have electricity here."

She looked at the cloudy sky. "Hopefully, it stays that way. I can't help it if the grid goes down."

He glanced up and frowned. "How about I start a fire just in case?"

"And you owe me your special hot cocoa."

He took her overnight bag and led the way into the house. "I'm not a barista, but I can mix powder and boiling water."

She looked at him with her mouth open. "You're making me instant cocoa?" She swiped her bag from his hand and pretended like she was leaving. "I'll camp on a cot at Doc's clinic." She took a step toward the door when his hand came out and touched her shoulder.

"I'll doctor it up. You'll like it, I promise."

She would never have left, but it was nice that he wanted her to stay. "Okay, deal. How about I make a fire, and you make the cocoa?"

"You know how to make a fire?"

A *pffft* sound rolled from her mouth. "Oh, please. If I can use a table saw, man a drill, and install a new breaker box, I can certainly make a fire."

"Then get to it." He laughed and walked into the kitchen.

This house was a mirror image of his, and she also considered tearing out the wall separating the kitchen from the living room. She loved the great room concept because it was inclusive. She tossed her bag into the corner by the door and walked to the fireplace. With the weather turning, it was the first thing she made sure worked. How many times did she watch the news and see people freezing in their homes because they planned poorly?

Just thinking about how cold she would've been in her apartment sent a shiver down her spine.

She found a newspaper on the table. "Can I use your paper?"

He poked his head around the kitchen door. "Yep, and I already brought in some firewood. There was a nice-sized stack by the back door. I was planning on building a fire tonight, anyway. Lighter is on the mantel."

She scrunched up a few pages of newspaper and found smaller pieces of wood to use for the kindling. She started the flame and watched the smoke snake up and disappear into the flue.

"Do you like cinnamon?"

"In my hot cocoa?"

"No, in general?"

"Sure, I like it." As the flame grew larger and hotter, she added a log, then another, until the dried bark of the wood crackled. She shifted the metal screen into place and stood up.

"Fire is going; where's that cocoa?"

"Demanding, aren't you?"

"I've been told, but the truth is I have standards."

He handed her a cup of cocoa that didn't look like it was instant. Billowing on top of the dark rich chocolate was a dollop of whipped cream sprinkled with cinnamon.

She'd never had cinnamon with her chocolate but couldn't say it didn't taste good because it did.

"Yummy." She licked the whipped topping from her lip. "There's something else in here too."

He smiled. "Nope, that's it, but I made it with milk instead of water."

"It's all in the details."

"That it is." He shuffled to the sofa and flopped down. "Have a seat and tell me what you're going to do with this place."

She took the end of the couch opposite him. The fire burned to her left. "Working on your house has given me some ideas. I like the open-floor concept and will probably tear down that wall." She thumbed over her shoulder toward the kitchen. "I love the way it makes the entire house seem inviting."

"Opens it up and makes the area look bigger."

She kicked off her boots, and they hit the floor with a thunk. With her socked feet tucked under her bottom, she turned to face him. "I figure this house is the same as yours, so it's been great practicing on yours."

He laughed. "Perfect, make your mistakes on the house next door."

She tugged a throw he had draped over the couch and pulled it across her lap. "I don't make mistakes."

He lifted a brow as if to challenge her. "I believe you. I haven't seen you make one yet."

She resisted the urge to roll her eyes. "Okay, I've made a few mistakes."

"Do tell."

They spent the next hour talking about the episodes where she blundered. Nothing as severe as the load-bearing wall collapsing, but she'd had a few mishaps. Once she'd connected the water wrong, and the toilets were steaming. Another time she installed a set of windows backward, and they opened from the outside.

"What does the show do when things go wrong?"

"Usually, we fix it and then film again."

He cocked his head. "But not the show that ruined your career?"

"There was too much to fix. Once the wall gave way, the kitchen collapsed, and something shorted, and the house caught fire. By the time it was said and done, there wasn't much left."

"I don't know why they even aired that show."

Thinking about it made her stomach ache. "They needed to wrap it up, and it turns out the producer needed me out of the picture because she was pregnant."

He scooted toward the middle and placed his hand on her covered knee. It was an intimate show of affection, but he wasn't trying to seduce her. He attempted to comfort her. How she thought him a slimeball, she couldn't fathom. He'd been nothing but kind and sincere.

"You once said she was your best friend, but you always call her the producer."

It was silly, but giving her a name made it seem more real, and it was a time in her life she would've liked to forget.

"You ever see the *Harry Potter* movies? She's like Voldemort, that which shall never be named."

"But you just named him."

"That's because Voldemort can't hurt me."

"Neither can she."

He was right. She'd already done the damage. "Her name is Sylvia, and we met when she brought me onto the show. They had already chosen Matt, and I think she had a thing for him then. It's an unnatural situation when you're thrust into a situation where you live and breathe your work. You find a connection with people you wouldn't normally give the time of day to."

"I know a little something about that."

She hated to razz him about his upbringing, but he was obviously Bentleys and boarding schools.

"Must be awful to have every privilege known to man."

"You'd think it was amazing, but it was a trap. I liken it to being part of the royal family. You were born into something most people would think a fairy tale, but your life doesn't belong to you. You're a chess piece in a complex game."

"What, did Buffy turn you down for prom?"

He chuckled. "Her name was Charity, and she went with me."

She leaned forward and set her empty mug on the coffee table. "Was she?"

He got up and put another log on the fire. "Was she what?"

She felt like a teen trying to get her best friend to kiss and tell. "Charitable?"

"A gentleman never says."

"I'm not sure I'd go that far. Oh, to be a fly on the locker room wall of the high school gym."

"Smells like sweat and bad attitudes. I swear testosterone smells like a skunk."

She covered her mouth and yawned. "Sorry, the day is catching up to me."

"You work hard. Let's get you into bed." He rose and walked to where her bag sat in the corner. "I can sleep on the couch."

She rolled off the couch, folded the blanket, and laid it over the back of the sofa. "You don't have to. We're both adults, and I'm positive we can control ourselves."

"I put the bed in the master since it had its own bathroom."

She moved down the hallway to the first bedroom and turned right. The king-sized bed was a tight fit, leaving just enough room on each side for a nightstand, and on the large wall across from the bed was his dresser.

"What side do you want?" he asked.

"I don't care. I can sleep on either." She usually worked herself into exhaustion each day, so once she hit the mattress, she was out in seconds, but something told her tonight would be different. She hadn't slept with a man in a very long time, and knowing he was there just inches from her made her a little nervous.

"Okay, I'll take the side closest to the door."

That warmed her heart. Her mother once told her you could tell a man's character by what side of the bed he chose. A man who puts himself between you and the door is a protector. She always thought it was a bunch of nonsense, but then she married Matt, and he slept farthest from the door. He never walked into the house first to make sure it was safe, and he didn't pull her behind him when danger approached.

"What's that smile on your face?" he asked.

She set her bag on the bed and pulled out her flannel PJs. "Never thought the first time I'd be back in bed with a man would be like this."

He moved with stealth toward her. "It can be any way you want it to be. You want more?"

Her insides churned with need. "What I want and what's wise is a different story."

He tipped her chin and looked into her eyes. "Last time I took the kiss, next time you'll have to."

He stepped back and pulled off his shirt, displaying that perfectly honed body that she found herself longing to feel again.

"I'll get ready." She stared at him for another few seconds before she swiped up her nightclothes and toothbrush and dashed toward the bathroom.

She closed herself inside and leaned on the door. "What the hell are you thinking." She said out loud.

"What was that?"

"Nothing," she moved to the sink to brush her teeth. *Get your mind off him.* The more she tried to banish him from her thoughts, the more she thought of him and that kiss and how his cologne seemed to float around her constantly.

She changed into her flannel pajamas because they were the least sexy thing she had to wear, and she chose them for that reason.

She resisted the urge to brush her hair, pink her

cheeks, and slick on lip gloss. She wasn't entering that room for any other reason than sleep.

When she walked out, she found him standing at the foot of the bed wearing only boxer briefs and a smile.

"I normally don't sleep in anything, but I'll cover up for you." He turned to face her, leaving nothing to her imagination.

Not true, there was plenty she imagined, but it wouldn't happen. She feigned indifference and hoped the heat she felt on her cheeks didn't betray her. "Wear what you want. You don't have anything I haven't seen before."

"True, but you haven't seen mine."

This time she let her eyes roll back in exaggeration. "Whatever. You've seen one, and you've seen them all."

"Says the girl whose cheeks are as red as the cherry pie filling."

"Oh my God, we didn't eat the pie." She was ready to bolt into the kitchen.

"We'll *devour* it tomorrow."

The way he said devour made her core heat. It was a feeling she thought had abandoned her when her husband did, but it was back and strong.

"Night." She pulled down the navy-blue comforter and slipped between the softest sheets she'd ever felt. An uncontrollable hum left her.

"Now, that sound will get you in trouble."

He walked to the bathroom but stopped at the doorway.

"Nice sheets."

"Makes you want to stay in bed and do naughty things, right?"

"Nope. It makes me want to sleep." She turned over, giving him her back so he couldn't see the look on her face. She knew if he saw her eyes, he'd notice the hunger there.

How in the hell was she going to get through this night?

# CHAPTER THIRTEEN

*How am I supposed to get through the night?* Mason glanced down at the sleeping body curled up next to him. He'd shifted as far as he could to the edge of the bed until he was on the verge of falling off.

Each time he put distance between them, she sought his heat and scooted in to snuggle. Inch by inch, he moved from the edge until his entire body was back on the bed. That was when she threw an arm and leg over him and trapped him beside her. There was no fighting it. He let out an exhale and relaxed. Well, maybe not fully relaxed because his body had different ideas than his mind.

It wasn't like she was naked. She wore granny flannels buttoned up to her chin, but damn she was cute. His baser self didn't care if she was wrapped in foil, tied with twine, and bagged like a takeout lunch.

She pressed against him.

"The universe hates me," he whispered.

As if she heard his words, she sighed and pressed her body more tightly to his. Her hand came to rest over his heart. There was no use fighting it. He craved her heat, too, so he wrapped his arm around her shoulder and tugged her closer. Morning would come soon enough, and the experience would be over. For now, he'd enjoy the embrace and the heat her body gifted him.

---

HE WOKE to a thump on his chest.

"Let me go."

He bolted upright, tossing her off his body like she was as light as a feather because she couldn't have weighed much.

"What's wrong?" He stood at the side of the bed, hands fisted to protect her from whatever was coming. "What happened?"

With her eyes narrowed and lips pulled into a thin line, she pointed at him. "You, you happened. I knew you couldn't keep to our bargain. You had me trapped in a bear hug. You were supposed to stay on your side of the bed." She stomped her foot for effect, but it made no sound.

He stared at her for a moment. "Are you serious?" He pointed to the bed where the covers were only mussed on his side. It was as if she'd slid over like she was air, and the covers settled back into place. "You were on my side. All night I moved away until I had no space left, then I just gave in and let you sleep beside me."

Her mouth dropped open. "You gave in." She made a cute little huff. "As if sleeping next to me is such a hardship."

While her response was definitive, there was a question in her eyes and something else that looked like hurt.

He darted like a rocket toward her and pulled her against his chest. "You are no one's hardship," he whispered. "I just didn't want this to happen. I would've gladly held you all night, but you made it clear that we had boundaries. Obviously, your body didn't get the memo." He kissed her hair and stepped back a couple of inches.

She took that moment to stare at the bed again. "Should I be apologizing to you?" She looked up at him like a child would a parent when they're in trouble.

He shook his head. "No, best night of sleep I've had in a long time." He cleared his throat. "Well ...

after I ignored that there was a hot flannel-dressed woman draped over my body."

She ran her hands down her sides. "Not the sexiest thing in the world."

He chuckled. "I don't know. I thought it was pretty hot. Not designed to seduce, but hey, everyone has their thing, and I guess mine is flannel."

A smile twitched at the corner of her lips until she couldn't contain it any longer, and then it pulled her lips wide and lit up her eyes.

"You're crazy."

He shrugged. "Maybe." He strode toward her until his bare chest touched her flannel shirt. He was about to do something he might regret, but he knew he'd regret it more if he didn't. "I know I said I'd wait for you to kiss me, but I can't, and I'm not sorry." He lowered his head and brushed his lips tentatively against hers. If he felt any resistance, he'd step back. Instead, her hand cupped the back of his head, and she tugged him closer.

Her velvety tongue swept out to taste his lips, and he opened them for her. The touch of their tongues was like an electrical charge flowing through him.

"So damn hot," he whispered against her lips.

"You are so not my type," she said against his.

"Good," he nipped at her lower lip. "Your type sucks for you."

She let out a moan that he was sure was an admission of truth. They stood and kissed for what seemed like a lifetime, and then she shuffled back and touched her fingers to her lips.

"Wow." She took in several deep breaths. "Wow."

He smiled. "You already said that."

"Yep ... wow." She picked up her bag and moved past him into the bathroom. "So that you know," she called from the other side of the door. "I expect breakfast after I sleep with a man."

The laugh started deep in his belly and trickled up to his chest. "I've made you breakfast all week."

She opened the door and peeked out. "I know, so why should this be any different."

He didn't know why, but it was. "How about those cheese blintzes you wanted?" He'd put in an order for the ingredients yesterday and had them delivered. It wasn't a cheap delivery from Copper Creek, but if the smile on her face was the reward, it was already worth it.

"You keep feeding me like that, and I may never leave."

*I hope you don't.*

He didn't know where that thought came from, but it was true. He'd never been so out of sorts and yet felt so in touch with who he was.

"I'll use the other bathroom to shower, and then I'll get started on breakfast."

"Chop, chop," she teased. "We've got stuff to do."

She ducked back into the bathroom and closed the door.

He got a change of clothes and made his way to the hallway bathroom.

Twenty minutes later, he was in the kitchen making coffee and following an internet recipe for cheese blintzes when she appeared like the sunshine. Her very presence lit up a room and made it feel warm.

"I got cherry and blueberry topping. Which do you want?"

She puckered out her lips, which only made him want to kiss them again.

"Can I have both? I mean ... why have only one when there are two."

He loved that she was a woman with an appetite. His last girlfriend was impossible to eat with. She was vegan and only ate low glycemic index veggies, so basically, she devoured kale by the pound. Eating out was impossible, which was why he'd learned to cook. Steamed kale wasn't his thing, so he was in charge if he wanted flavor, or texture, or protein.

"You want a cup of coffee?" It was the first thing he started when he got to the kitchen.

"I'll get it. You keep blintzing. I'm starving."

"Glad to hear it."

He made the crepe-like layer, filled it with the ricotta cheese mixture, rolled it, and then topped it off with fruit pie filling before sprinkling it with powdered sugar.

"Next time, I'll make the fruit topping myself."

"You look comfortable in the kitchen."

He moved around the space like it was his domain, but then again, he always felt safe and at ease in the kitchen because of Heidi.

"I spent a lot of time in the kitchen as a kid. My parents traveled, so Heidi, our housekeeper, slash cook, slash nanny, slash surrogate parent, took care of me. She was an excellent cook. You should taste my schnitzel and spaetzle. It's to die for."

She laughed. "When are we having it?" She leaned against the counter and sipped her coffee. They were back to their morning routine. He could see doing this every day with her because it was so comfortable and felt right.

"How about Friday? I need to make an order."

"You're getting your food from someone else?" She looked aghast.

"You might not have what I need."

"I'll order what you need, and it will be here Thursday. Make a list."

"I didn't know." He never imagined he could special order things from The Corner Store.

"You never asked."

He finished her plate and put it on the table. "If I ask, can I have whatever I want?" He moved closer to her.

She set her mug on the counter and closed the gap between them. "What do you want?"

"You." He covered her mouth with a scorching kiss. By the time it was over, he was sure her breakfast was cold, but she didn't seem to mind.

"Oh my God, these are great." She devoured the two blintzes and asked for more, which he gladly made.

He sat with her once he finished the second batch and had to admit they were tasty. "What's on the agenda today?"

"Bathroom demo. We're gutting the whole thing."

He let her take the reins with the project. She knew the budget and chose only what he could sell. The hardest thing would be finding a buyer because not everyone was looking at living in the small town of Aspen Cove, Colorado.

"What are you thinking as far as the shower and bath? Right now, it's the standard tub-shower combo. Do you think that's the way to go?" He was hoping she'd do something different.

She reached for the pen and paper on the table. "I was going to ask if we could do a shower with a bench in the master and then have a soaking tub in the hallway bathroom. There isn't room for both in the master bath, and we don't have the budget to expand."

He fisted the air. "Yes! I was hoping you'd do something different."

"All you have to do is ask."

"I didn't want to overstep."

She reached over the table and stole his last bite of the cherry blintz.

"It's your house and your money." She popped the bite into her mouth, chewed, and swallowed. "Besides, it was part of our deal. I'd help you refurbish, and I got a steal of a deal on this place." She smiled.

"True, but I am staying in your house rent-free while you refurb my mess next door."

She set her fork down and leaned back in the chair, rubbing her stomach. "You're paying in blintzes."

"It's my pleasure."

"Should we clean up and go?" She rose and placed her plate in the sink.

He moved in behind her, trapping her between his arms, her back to his front. "I like this whole domestic thing with you."

She leaned back. "You're not so bad. I'll keep you around for your cooking skills."

He nuzzled her neck. "That's only until I show you my other skills."

She spun around and faced him. "Oh, can you make a good hollandaise?"

Before he could kiss her again, she ducked under his arm and escaped his hold.

"Baby, I can make anything if motivated properly."

She giggled. "Is this a negotiation?"

"It can be. What are you offering?"

She sashayed forward, her hips swaying with each step. "I'd do just about anything for eggs Benedict," she cooed. When she reached him, she lifted on her tiptoes and planted a kiss smack dab on his lips. "Now, let's go. We're on a short timeline to your trust fund."

"Right. Let's do this."

The funny thing was, he'd thought very little of it since they started working together. He mostly thought about how fulfilling the renovation was and how working side by side with the right person could make a job feel less like torture and more like pure pleasure. At the end of the day, he was exhausted, but it was a good feeling to know he'd earned that fatigue through hard work and not manipulation. With his father, there was always an angle, but with Jewel, it was always straightforward. He could see the fruits of his labor, and that was a satisfying experience.

She moved to the door and opened it, then froze. A flash went off and then another.

"JJ Monroe," a male voice called out. "Is this where you've been hiding?"

Mason stepped in front of her as the reporter continued his questions, and the photographer continued to snap pictures.

"You're on private property. Leave." He kept his tone even and calm because he knew everything he said would become tomorrow's headline.

"I told you," Jewel cried. "Your father was up to something, and you said he wasn't. You were probably in on it."

She moved him aside and slammed the door.

All he could think about was, how was he going to fix this?

# CHAPTER FOURTEEN

He felt the reverberation of the slamming door in his bones.

"I told you." Jewel stomped toward the living room and flopped onto the couch. "That's your father's doing."

He shook his head. "You can't be sure." He moved to squat in front of her, setting his hands on her knees. "He's not even in town."

"He doesn't have to be in town."

Her voice verged on hysteria, making him see how much the idea of press coverage affected her.

"Well, he isn't. He's in the Maldives with Sable."

Her head rolled back on the cushions, and she stared at the ceiling. "Ever heard of *the internet?*" She crossed her arms over her chest with a huff, then looked over her shoulder to the door. "There's a photographer and a reporter outside."

He stood and walked to the window. After peeking through the blinds, he let out a low whistle. "It's more like a few crews."

She hopped up and raced to where he stood. "Oh. My. God."

He let the blind go and set his hands on her shoulders. "Hey, look at me." When she finally met his eyes, he continued. "Did you think you could hide out forever?"

Her chin fell toward her chest, but he thumbed it up, forcing her to face him. "Yes, I figured I'd have more time. They hounded me for months."

"How did you get away from them then?" He always wondered how she escaped their notice.

Her lips pursed. "I packed a bag and left in the middle of the night."

"You brought nothing here but a suitcase?"

"And my car." She shook her head. "Actually, I traded my car in and got the Cayenne."

He pulled her in for a hug and chuckled. "If you were trying to blend in, buying an orange Porsche SUV probably wasn't the way to go."

She leaned into him, and he closed his arms around her, hugging her tightly.

"It had good safety ratings."

"So does an Acura or a Lexus but a Porsche?"

She pulled back, but he didn't let her go. "I liked the color, and it drives like it's on rails."

He laughed. "All right, *Pretty Woman,* you were letting your inner Julia Roberts out, I get it, but what's done is done. They know you're here, so what are you going to do about it?"

Releasing his hold was hard because she felt so perfect in his embrace, but the press wasn't going anywhere, and they needed a plan.

"How long do you think it'll take to tunnel under the two houses?"

"Let me make us another cup of coffee, and we'll look at the house plans." He knew she wasn't serious, but they needed a strategy. Somehow he had to convince her to stay on board. Without her, the house would never get finished, and he'd lose the thirty-five million.

While he put on the coffee, she took a seat at the kitchen table.

"You have two choices; you can work against them or work with them. The thing about the press is the harder you push back, the more they try to infiltrate. Why not give them unfettered access to the project?"

"You'd like that wouldn't you?"

"This isn't about me. It's about you." He got the creamer out of the refrigerator and put a teaspoon of sugar in her cup.

"It might be about me, but the press won't hurt you at all. For all I know, you tipped them off."

"For all you know, I did, but the truth is, I didn't." He poured a splash of cream into her coffee and started his. "How would it serve me if you quit the project? I know how media averse you are. Why would I sabotage myself?"

She leaned forward and gently pounded her head on the table.

"Stop, or you'll give yourself a concussion, and then where will I be?" He handed her the coffee and doctored his before taking a seat across from her.

"What am I going to do?" Her eyes grew wide as she looked past him to the back door. When he turned, he saw the photographer aiming the camera in their direction. Mason jumped from his seat and yanked the curtains closed, leaving them in the dark until he flipped the switch.

"As I said, you have to decide if you're willing to give them something. Let me tell you, if you don't, they'll take what they want anyway."

"Oh, I know. They've gotten their pound of flesh from me. Haven't I given enough?"

He rubbed his chin. It broke his heart that she was in this situation. Looking at how pale she turned and how her hands shook as she raised the mug for a sip twisted his gut.

"Yes, you've probably given enough, but they're a hungry bunch whose appetite is never satisfied."

They sat in silence for several minutes.

"I think I could tunnel under my house to yours. It would put us behind schedule but solve a lot of problems."

It was a joke, but getting behind schedule was no laughing matter.

"I don't have time to tunnel. You know I have a deadline." He hadn't considered that she might leave the project. There was nothing but a handshake keeping her there. He'd already signed over the house so she could easily walk away for the renovation and wash her hands of the press. "Are you going to quit on me?" It was a real possibility.

He stared at her in anticipation. The longer he waited for the answer, the stronger his heart beat. He was certain it would crack the cage surrounding it.

"I'm no quitter." She took another drink of coffee and set her mug down. "I'm not giving in to them either. I'll ignore them, and maybe they'll go away."

He shook his head. "Did they before?"

"No, but maybe I didn't hold out long enough."

"Six months wasn't long enough for them to lose interest. Then why do you think it would be now. You're like Waldo, and they've finally found you. Do you think for a moment they're going to let you out of their sight?"

She worried her lower lip, chewing and gnawing until it was plump and red. If they were in any other situation than this one, he'd consider kissing those luscious lips. Truth be told, he'd considered kissing them a lot—all night long. He had to get his mind off the way her body felt tucked next to his and focus on the crisis at hand. The minutes seemed to pass by quickly, and the one thing he didn't have was time. He wasn't sure if he'd be able to get the house finished, on the market, and sold before he met his deadline.

"I say we make a run for it. We can lock ourselves inside and get to work. Today is bathroom demo day, right? Let's take some of your frustration out on the tile and that awful tub." The tub was more of a slate gray that used to be white. He didn't understand how porcelain could lose its luster and turn the color of pigeon poop, but it did.

"Okay."

Joy rushed through his veins. He didn't expect her to give in so easily.

"Okay?"

She nodded. "I made a promise, and I'll keep it. You're counting on me, and without you, I wouldn't have this house, which by the way, is rather nice." She hugged herself. "I can't believe the first night I stayed in it, and I had to sleep with you." She rose from the chair and took her mug to the sink. "You snore."

"I do not." He hardly slept. How was it possible he snored?

"You do." She moved past him and cupped his cheek. "Like a freight train."

"Well, you make these little mewling sounds like a kitten purring."

"I do not."

He wrapped his arm around her shoulders and led her to the door. "You do. If you sound like that when you're sleeping ..." He let his head roll back and closed his eyes. "I can only imagine what sounds you make when you—"

He opened the door and rushed her out.

"When I what?" She stared at him as he pushed past the photographers and reporters blocking the porch.

His plan was working. All he needed to do was distract her, and once they were next door, she'd be fine.

In the background, voices called out questions like, "Is he your boyfriend? How long did you think you could hide? Is this your new project?"

"Answer the question," she said, still staring at him as he pushed through the front door of his house. When he closed it behind him, he turned to look at her. "What question?"

"Oh my god, you distracted me."

"I did, and it worked." Feeling like he'd accomplished some Herculean task, he smiled. "Did you say you wanted to start on the bathrooms?"

"Do I make noises when I sleep?"

He leaned in and brushed his lips against hers. "Yes, and they drove me insane all night."

Her grin warmed him through. Some people smiled, and it was just nice, and then some lit up a room when their lips lifted. Jewel was a bright light when she grinned. She could turn an apocalypse into a fairy tale with her smile.

"Good, because you drive me insane too." She pressed a quick kiss to his mouth and started for the hallway. "Master or hall bathroom?" she asked.

"The master still has blinds."

"Smart thinking." She picked up the sledgehammer and led the way. "Time to do some damage."

He watched as she entered the bathroom, put on her safety goggles, and took the first swing. There was anger at the end of that hammer. All he could think about was how unfortunate it'd be if she turned that anger on him.

She spent the morning destroying the bathroom.

By noon she looked exhausted, standing in the center of a pile of rubble. Sweat glistened from her forehead, but a look of satisfaction gave her a glow.

"I'm starving. What about Maisey's for lunch?"

She brushed off her hands and shook the dust from her hair.

"You know they'll be waiting outside and follow you everywhere."

"I'm not going to starve to death because they want a story. There's no story to be had. Let's go."

He stood there with a slack jaw. "What happened to you?" Just that morning, she was cowering in the kitchen, and now she was ready to face them?

"I beat the hell out of the bathroom."

"Okay, then." He didn't know what her plan was, but he was about to see. "Do you want me to drive?"

"Yep, your car is closer."

He tapped his pocket to make sure his keys were there.

"Maisey's it is."

At the front door, she took several breaths and lifted her shoulders before swinging it open and walking outside.

The press clambered toward her, and she moved forward as if she didn't see them.

Mason was sure they didn't expect her to walk out the door, nor were they prepared for it, so it gave her time to round his SUV and climb inside. That sent several of them racing to their cars so they could follow.

"Amazing."

"What?"

"How you played them."

"I didn't play them, I'm just hungry, and if something got in my way, I was ready to go to battle because it's meatloaf day at Maisey's, and I'd kill for that."

He backed out of the driveway and headed for Main Street.

It didn't take long for the crew following them to catch on to where they were going. He pulled into the closest empty parking spot, and she was out of the car before he even came to a complete stop.

"Meet you inside," she said.

When he entered the diner, he found her sitting in the corner booth opposite the one Doc usually sat in. Her back was to the door. She seemed to take the stance: *what she can't see won't hurt her.* Sadly, that wasn't always true.

He plopped onto the red fake leather bench and watched the press scurry like insects into the restaurant.

"I wondered how long it would take them to find you," Maisey said. She turned over both coffee cups and poured. "Start with this, and I'll be back." She stared at Jewel. "Blue plate today, sweetheart?"

Jewel gaped at her. "You knew who I was?"

Maisey laughed. "Honey, we have cable and eyes. Everyone knows who you are. We were waiting for you to figure it out." She walked away, but he heard her tell the news crew if they were taking up her tables, they were paying her rent.

"I told you so." The more he looked at Jewel's shocked expression, the harder he laughed. How did she ever think she could be invisible?

# CHAPTER FIFTEEN

So far, ignoring the press was working. If she didn't engage with them, it was almost as if they weren't there. Almost except for their constant shouts and the cameraman who was always sticking the lens in her face.

It tempted her to actually earn the nickname Wreck-It Rita and tear the thing from his hand so she could take her sledgehammer to it, but she didn't want to borrow trouble.

"New vanity comes today," Mason sat at the kitchen table, going over the budget. "Did we need double sinks?"

He'd asked her that no less than a dozen times.

"Do you want to sell the house?"

He tossed the pen to the side and exhaled. "Yes, but I don't want to price myself out of the market."

She made a second cup of coffee for herself and sat across from him. "I don't understand why you didn't just sell both houses for a penny over the asking price. That technically is a profit."

He rubbed his chin and leaned back in the chair. "You're right, but you're not. It's a profit over the asking price. However, we've been holding on to these houses for years now, and the loans are accruing interest. When my father says profit, he means the homes have to make money after paying off the loans, including the hundred grand I'm using to refurb and the realtor fees. If I'm lucky, I'll make a penny once I pay those."

She hadn't considered the bind he might be in. She focused on the renovation, not the cost.

"We can cut costs on the tile and flooring, but double sinks are a must. People divorce over less. Have you ever had to share a single sink bathroom with a woman?"

He lifted a brow. She loved how expressive his eyes were. "I've been sharing a bathroom with you all week."

"Sure, but I'm low-maintenance."

Up came his other brow. "You are not. I see all the crap you put on your face at night."

She opened her mouth to refute, but it was no

use. She had a routine, and it had several parts that started with a specific face wash and ended with a very expensive moisturizer.

"That crap keeps me looking youthful."

"You are youthful." He reached for her hand. "And you're beautiful."

"Thank you."

They'd been sleeping together for several days now. After meatloaf at Maisey's, she snuck out the back door and entered her store from the alley. Sadly, the hard freeze and water destroyed the floor of her home, and until she could make time to tear it out, she was stuck sleeping with Mason.

If she were honest with herself, she didn't mind climbing into bed with him at night. They did their best to stay on opposite sides of the mattress, but somehow she always woke up on his side of the bed with Mason wrapped around her, and it just felt right.

"I need you to buckle down on the costs because things are tight, and if I run out of money, I won't be able to make those eggs Benedict you want."

"Are you flirting with me?"

"Maybe."

"Let's go to work." She set her mug inside the sink and walked to the front door. It was getting to be routine, pushing past the reporters and photographers who seemed to multiply like bunnies in the spring. Every once in a while, she'd stop and smile so they could catch a photo that didn't have her frowning.

She opened the door expecting the same but stopped dead in her tracks when she came face-to-face with Matt and Sylvia.

The flashes went off like firecrackers, no doubt catching her shock.

"What are you doing here?" She swallowed the lump that rose in her throat. It was a fiery ball of rage churning inside, just waiting to be lobbed at the two people who had betrayed her.

"Can we talk?" Matt asked. He raised his hand, and the flashes stopped. He was like Moses, and the photographers were the Red Sea. He commanded it. So be it.

"I have nothing to say." She pushed past them and walked across the driveway, making her way to the other house.

"I have a lot to say, and it starts with I'm sorry."

She nearly tripped over her steel-toed boots. Matt had an extensive vocabulary, but I'm sorry was never part of his vernacular.

She spun around toward him. "You're sorry? Are you sorry you destroyed me?"

He sauntered up to her and leaned in. "Can we go inside and talk?"

A giggle bubbled inside her and came out sounding like a cackle.

"Now? You want to talk now." She waved her hand through the air. "The time for talking was a year ago. Where was your voice then?"

"Come on, JJ." It burned her up that he tried to use that sexy voice to get what he wanted. "That's in the past."

She shook her head. "I'm still living it." She pointed to the crowd of reporters standing there, waiting for the big story to erupt. "Haven't you seen the headlines?"

She had. She looked at them each morning. Today's news was, "Demolition Barbie is at it Again, but Will The Walls Come Tumbling Down Like Last Time?"

"I'd say it's time for redemption." He tilted toward her like he was going to kiss her, and she stumbled back into Mason, who caught her before she fell.

"Let's take this inside before we make tonight's news," Mason said. "I can see it now," he holds up his hands like he's unfolding a marquee. "Wreck-It Rita gets in the last swing and bludgeons her rotten ex with a sledgehammer."

"Hey man," Matt moved forward like a pit bull, ready to fight. "You don't know me."

"I don't need to. I know her, and I believe that what she says is true."

If she didn't already like him, she would've fallen

for Mason right there. He didn't require proof of anything. Her word was as good as gold. They weren't even in a relationship, and he trusted her. She trusted him, too, and it was that trust she should've received from a loving husband.

"I trusted you, and you screwed me over," she said to Matt as she moved past Mason and into the house. He was right. If they were going to air their dirty laundry, it shouldn't be in a public forum. "Come in and let's get this over with."

The four of them walked inside, and she looked at her work through their eyes. It had been a long time since she'd worked for Sylvia or beside Matt. It shouldn't have mattered what they thought, but it did. To have them validate her skills was a step in the right direction. A kind of redemption she was looking for. The funny thing is, she wasn't sure she needed it until right that second.

"Wow," Sylvia said. She kneeled to run her hands over the herringbone pattern on the floor. "It's beautiful, JJ."

"Jewel, my name is Jewel." She was no longer on good terms with these people. They all got screwed—Sylvia by Matt and Jewel by both of them. Somehow, Matt came out smelling like roses instead of the manure he was. "Why are you here?"

"To apologize," Matt said. He shuffled back and forth on his feet, a sure sign of his discomfort and his dishonesty. It was the same dance he did the day he swore the inspector came and said it wasn't a load-bearing wall.

"Bullshit. Why are you here?" She glanced at Mason, who signaled to the door as if asking her if she wanted him to leave. She shook her head because she needed his support.

He grabbed a few five-gallon buckets and brought them into the living room, where they all took a seat. Outside, reporters bobbed and bounced, taking shots through the windows as they saw fit. She would've put blinds up already, but Mason kept reminding her that the budget was tight.

"Ratings are down since you left," Sylvia said.

"That's a shame." She rubbed her chin like she was deep in thought. "I always thought I was the brains, and you were the beefcake." She glanced at Mason and smiled. "Maybe I was the beauty after all."

He returned her smile. "You are beautiful."

Matt pointed at her, then Mason. "Are you two a thing?" He snorted. "He's so not your type."

Jewel laughed. "Oh, you mean a lousy, no good, cheating, lying bastard? I'm over that." She scooted closer to Mason. "I like a man with morals."

"Right," Sylvia said. "Let's get to the point."

Jewel couldn't help but notice the chasm of space

between Sylvia and Matt. The divide was wide enough to push a six-burner stove through.

"Yes," Jewel said, leaning against Mason's shoulder. "Let's move it along. We have work to do."

"As the producer of *Reno or Wreck It*, we'd love it if you'd rejoin the team."

The floor dropped out from under her, and she squeezed Mason's arm so tightly he winced.

"Are you insane?" She hopped to her feet, overturning the bucket. "You come into my house." She looked around. "Actually, his house, and you ask me to come back to save your asses?"

Matt stood and walked toward her, stopping out of her reach, which was a good thing because she had an uncontrollable urge to choke him.

"Think of this as a win-win. You get to redeem yourself, and we get a boost in ratings."

The cackle was back, only this time she didn't suppress it. It rang through the empty room like a warbling siren.

"You're serious."

"Hear us out," Sylvia said. "You get to show that you're the true talent."

Matt swung around to scowl at Sylvia.

"Well, she is. You were the beefcake. Sadly, all brawn and no brains."

Her brows shot up so hard it made them ache.

"Trouble in paradise?"

"I already filed annulment papers," Sylvia said.

Jewel glanced at Matt and then at Sylvia. "What about the baby?"

Sylvia shrugged. "False alarm."

"Down and out lie." Matt turned to Jewel. "Baby, I would've never left you if it wasn't for the baby."

Mason cleared his throat. "Maybe I should step out."

Jewel yelled, "No," at the same time, Matt yelled, "Yes!" She waved her hands in front of her face like she was directing traffic when all she wanted was silence. "Everybody be quiet." When the room stilled, she took several breaths to clear her thoughts.

"You're only here because you need me. Without me, the show gets canceled." She knew she was right because it was written all over their faces. "I'm your golden calf, and if you don't get me to sign on, you both lose your jobs."

"It's not that desperate," Matt said.

"Oh, don't let him fool you," Sylvia said. "It's dire. Yes, we need you."

She'd never been in such a position of power before, and while she should've loved it, she didn't. Their lives were in her hands, or at least their livelihood. The tables had turned, and she was in control.

"Where were you when I needed my best friend," she asked Sylvia. "Oh, that's right, you were sleeping with my husband."

She turned to Matt. "And where were you when I needed you to validate me? You were supposed to have my back." She shook her head and looked at Sylvia. "Did he cheat on you too?"

She knew he had the minute Sylvia's shoulders rolled forward. It was the look of the defeated.

"Yes, he got friendly with the intern."

"Did it hurt?" She knew the pain of betrayal. It was like a dull, rusty blade cutting through tender flesh.

"Very much."

With a nod, Jewel retook a seat. "Good. It's important to feel the pain you inflict on others. It might make you think twice about how you behave in the future."

She turned her head to face Matt.

"Will you come back to the show?"

She shook her head. "No way." She pointed to the door. "I think it's time for you to leave. Mason and I have work to do."

"We'll pay for the rest of the renovation cost, and we'll guarantee a sale."

Mason's eyes popped wide. "You'll guarantee a sale?"

"Mason," Jewel warned. "No."

He tossed his hands in the air and walked out of the room.

"Trouble in paradise?" Matt asked.

"Nope, we're independent islands. No paradise here. I'm simply helping." She shuffled him to the door.

"What's in it for you."

"Redemption." She opened the door, and as soon as they cleared the threshold, she slammed it shut.

When Mason appeared, she held up her hand. "I don't want to hear it." She felt bad for shutting him down, but she knew if he pressed, she would say yes because they offered her everything she wanted. She'd get a chance to prove her talent and leave the show with her ego intact. It didn't escape her that Mason would get what he needed too. They would finish the house in time because they'd have access to a team and there was the guaranteed sale of the home. All of it sounded great, but did she want to save Sylvia and Matt? The answer was no.

# CHAPTER SIXTEEN

Was Jewel insane? They served everything she wanted on a silver platter, and she tossed it away. All this time, she talked about redemption when what she really wanted was the other R-word—revenge.

He tossed broken tiles into the five-gallon bucket and wondered if he'd get the house done in time.

"Are you mad at me?" she asked.

He continued to throw the debris into the bin. "No." That was the truth. He understood where she was coming from. They had destroyed her life, and now they were back looking to her as their savior. "I get why you said no, but isn't that what you wanted? You wanted redemption. You wanted to leave the show with your head held high."

She leaned against the wall and sighed. "True,

but I don't want them to control me or the situation, and they will, you know it. I'll be the lion in their circus, and they'll crack the whip."

Mason's phone rang. Not recognizing the number, he answered it like he did all business calls. "Mason Van der Veen, how can I help you."

Someone on the other end of the line cleared their throat. "Mason," the familiar voice said. "This is Sylvia. Can you talk?"

She asked as if they were undercover lovers sneaking around. He imagined she had a lot of experience with that.

"What can I do for you?" He moved from the bathroom to the living room so Jewel could continue to work.

"It's what we can do for each other." She stalled for a moment. "You seem to have a close relationship with Jewel."

He didn't know what she was hinting at but felt protective of Jewel.

"We are strictly business partners."

"Yes," she said. "Elite Properties. You own a lot of houses in Aspen Cove that seem to sit without buyers. That's got to be costly."

He looked toward the bathroom and saw Jewel's shadow move against the wall. This conversation wasn't one he wanted to have in front of her. Something about it felt wrong, but he wanted to know where she was going. If anything, it would at least help him help Jewel, or that's what he told himself as he slipped outside into the backyard.

"You've done your homework."

She chuckled. "I've got people."

"I bet you do. Again, what can I do for you?"

"Get her to sign on. It's an easy decision. You've got a bunch of houses that need refurbing, and I've got the money and crew. We can help each other out here."

To him, it sounded like a dream situation. "What are you offering?" It wasn't like he could change Jewel's mind. She would do what she wanted to do.

"We've got a crew waiting to start. All I need is your okay and Jewel's participation. She can run the show. The house you're refurbing now will be the intro, and we'll take over the bathrooms and bedrooms since you've got the living room and kitchen under control. I'm offering you a sweet deal. You get your house done for free, and I guarantee a buyer even if it's the show that purchases the home."

His heart jackhammered in his chest. He was a deal away from his inheritance. All he needed to do was talk Jewel into it.

"What about the other houses? You brought them up."

"I did. I'm happy to sign a contract on the others, and as long as Jewel is part of the agreement, I'm handing you a guarantee. Surely, that would make Daddy happy."

Bringing up his father wasn't earning her his consent.

"This has nothing to do with my father."

She made a clucking sound. "I've got people, Mason. I know what's riding on the sale of the first house, and I'm willing to offer above your asking price so you can get your inheritance."

People inherently were gossipers, and the board was privy to the conversation, so keeping his situation a secret would never happen, but having it made public hurt.

He looked around him to make sure no one was listening. When the coast was clear, he said, "Basically, you're telling me that if I get Jewel to sign on to the deal, you'll buy my houses and give me a fair market value after refurbing them."

"Yes, let's call the refurb costs part of the contract —like renting production space. We'll refurb, stage, and show the house. All you have to do is dress nice and smile for the camera."

"And Jewel gets her redemption?"

"Jewel gets her show. No one is going to humiliate anyone on public TV. Neither Matt nor I will publicly apologize, but she can work and show that she has the skill."

"Hmm, not sure that will fly. You guys threw her under the bus."

"She should've double-checked the work. Though she took her husband's word for it, at the end of the day, it falls on her."

He couldn't argue with the logic, but she should've been able to trust Matt. They were a team, and as her husband, she should've been able to count on him.

He felt slimy having this conversation, but a part of him wanted it to happen. What would it cost Jewel? She'd gain far more than she lost. Sure, it benefitted him immensely as well, so he had a vested interest in getting her to say yes.

"It's a win-win," Sylvia said. "Can you convince her to say yes?"

"I don't know." He honestly couldn't say. They'd forged a friendship. To him, it seemed like things were heading in a different direction. They flirted and kissed and slept together. Each morning he woke with her wrapped in his arms. Their bodies knew what their brains refused to admit—they belonged together.

The selfish part of him wanted her to sign on and not only because it would help him out, but also, he enjoyed working with her. They moved like a well-oiled machine around each other. He wasn't a construction guy, but she always taught him the right way to do things. He'd learned so much from her. Maybe that's why the show was flopping. Jewel was the star and the teacher. She was the heartbeat, and without her, it flatlined.

"Will you try?"

That was the million-dollar question. No, it was the thirty-five-million-dollar question, and the answer was yes. He had to try. He'd be stupid not to.

"Yes. I'll try, but I make no guarantees. She'll do what's right for her in the end. If I get her to sign on, I'll need a separate guarantee that you'll sell the house in the next thirty days. The deal between us is between us."

"It's our secret."

He hated that word because its very nature was isolating. Very few secrets were good. They were skeletons that rattled behind closed doors.

"Fine, I'll figure it out."

"Have her call me directly when she comes back. And don't take too long because we are already behind schedule."

He hung up and took a few breaths. He'd like to think they were cleansing, but they were really for courage. Something about this felt wrong, but what choice did he have? They were behind schedule and over budget. Each day he felt his inheritance slipping out of his hands. There was no way he'd walk away from it if all it took was a yes from Jewel. As he went into the house, he thought of a thousand ways to ask her, but they all seemed underhanded. While he couldn't make the decision about him, he could ask her why she decided not to do it for her.

"Hey," he said as he entered the tight space. "Sorry about that. Real estate stuff." It wasn't a lie. He refused to lie to her.

"Oh, yeah?"

He nodded. "Someone was asking questions about the Aspen Cove properties."

"That's awesome. Did you offer to show them this one?"

He turned away from her. "They need it move-in ready right away."

A *thunk* sound came from the bucket, and he looked back at her. "I wish we had the budget to hire another set of hands."

He shrugged. This was his in, but the words stuck like dry sand in his mouth. He swallowed several times before he could speak.

"It's tight as it is. I'm not sure we'll have the budget to finish the house or the time to complete it." He slumped across the wall. "Too bad we don't have a crew like you did on the show." He knocked on the wooden framework. "We would whip this into shape in a day or so."

She huffed. "I know you think I'm silly for not doing it. It seems like a no-brainer. The Corner Store is doing fine with Beth running things. I'd be able to set the record straight. Maybe not by words, but by deeds. I'd earn a decent salary that I could use to fix up my place, and you'd get your inheritance."

He waved his hand in the air. "This isn't about me." It was, but she didn't have to know that. "Do what's best for you." He truly believed that, but deep inside, he wished she'd choose what was best for him too.

She tossed another tile into the bucket. "Here's the thing." She put a lid on the bucket and sat down. She seemed so small before him, even though her personality was usually larger than life. "If I go back, then it's like I'm giving in. This isn't about them or me wanting to do the right thing. This is them using me to get what they want. I have a problem with that."

He slid down the two-by-four and sat across from her. Her usually bright eyes were dull, and her skin wasn't pink with life and excitement. The entire ordeal had drawn the light from her.

"What if you twisted the situation to work for you? You can be in control here."

With her elbows on her knees, she fisted her hands and rested her chin on the flat of her knuckles.

"Not really. Sylvia will always be in control." Her lips turned up at the corners. "I'm glad he cheated on her too. Now she knows what it feels like." She leaned back and slapped her denim-clad knees. "After what she did, she wants me to save her ass."

His approach wasn't working. He didn't know how to twist this in her favor. "But what if by saving her ass, you realign yourself? This isn't about them. Remember that day you yanked the shelf down on my head." He raised a brow.

"I didn't yank it down." She turned so he couldn't see her face. "Okay, I may have pulled it, but I wasn't planning on it dropping on your head. I was after the commotion."

"You certainly got that." He rubbed at where the knot sat like an embedded egg on his forehead for days. "Why didn't you want anyone to know who you were?"

When she frowned, it took her whole face to make the look of disappointment from the curve of her lips to the crease on her brow.

"I was embarrassed."

"Same reason you don't want to face the press, right?"

Her head bobbed up and down. "They don't know the truth."

"This is your opportunity to tell the world the truth."

She sat taller as if his words were a steel rod giving her support.

"They would never let me tell the truth."

He was getting somewhere. "Maybe not, but you can use it as a learning tool. Turn it around and make it a lesson. This is why you don't leave the big stuff to the little people."

Her shoulders shook as laughter took over.

"Could you imagine? I can see Matt's face now as I look into the camera and call him little as in insignificant, or the worker bee instead of the king bee."

He knew he'd have her on the next thing he'd say.

"There aren't any king bees. It's always about the queen. Matt is just a drone. He only existed because of you. You don't have to get even. This isn't about revenge; it's a rebirth. You're the queen, and the hive belongs to you."

She cocked her head and smiled. "You know what? You're right. It was my show and my skills that made it a prime-time winner." She pulled her phone from her pocket. "I'm going to do it, but only because it's my choice. Not because someone manipulated me into it."

His stomach dropped and rebounded with a splash of acid that felt like a swarm of bees sought revenge at the back of his throat. What had he done?

# CHAPTER SEVENTEEN

She dialed the number and waited. It didn't take long for Sylvia to answer.

"Sylvia Monroe speaking, how may I help you? "

Hearing her say the last name stung, and Jewel considered hanging up. It was like pouring salt on an open wound or tearing a scab off a newly healed one.

"Monroe, huh?"

"Jewel? Is that you?"

She wanted to say, "wrong number," and hang up, but Mason was right. This was her chance at redemption. If the public could see her on the show again, they'd know she couldn't be that bad. Using it as a teachable moment was also smart. She could explain that it's always her job to dot the I's and cross the T's.

"It's me. Jewel *Monroe*." She emphasized her last name as if that validated ownership.

"Oh my God, I'm so glad you called. Does this mean that Ma... that maybe you changed your mind?"

"I have, but I have terms I must meet."

She heard Sylvia's muffled voice. "She's going to do it. Turn the car around and get the crew."

"Wait a minute. I said I have terms."

"Sure, sure, I get it."

"Do you get it because I don't think you do? You destroyed my career because you were selfish. Matt destroyed my reputation because he was too into you, literally, to care about the job."

Silence seemed to hang in the air like a storm cloud.

"I'm sorry. I am. Had I known what an asshole he was, I would've never been interested."

Jewel wanted to bang her head on the wall. "Do you hear yourself talking? He was married. That should've been the only roadblock you needed."

"You're right. I'm an awful person."

"Glad we agree. So, here's the deal. I'll do the show, but I won't do it with him. Mason will be my partner." She looked up just as he walked inside the room. "I know that he's not out to screw me over, and I can trust him."

"Hmm," Sylvia said, "Matt needs to be somewhere in the show. You know the ladies like to look at him."

Jewel thought about it for a second and knew Sylvia was right. He was the beefcake, the crew was the brawn, and she had always been the brain. Sylvia was nothing more than the banker turned bimbo.

"Fine, but I'm in charge, and if he so much as pisses me off once, I'm out."

"He'll be the angel the world thinks he is. Remember, our jobs are hanging on this, and we aren't stupid enough to mess it up."

"Debatable." She covered the phone and whispered to Mason.

"They're on their way back. I'll get you a good deal too."

"I'm not involved in that part of it. It's only my properties."

"Property as in one. It's a one and done, and they should pay you, too."

"Jewel?" Sylvia asked. "Are you there?"

"Yes, I want a ten percent raise and the same salary as mine for Mason."

"But he's not worth—"

"That's the deal, or there's none. You decide."

"Fine. You make the rules."

Jewel could hear the bitchiness in Sylvia's voice and gained some pleasure from her agreement. Usually, she was the one in charge, but not this time.

"Don't forget that. Now, as far as script ... I want it to be live."

"Do you think that's wise? I mean, with all the bad blood between you and Matt, there might be some fallout."

She thought back to her list and the fifty ways to murder her ex. None of them were on public television.

"It's my way or the highway."

"Right."

"See you soon."

Jewel hung up and threw herself into Mason's arms.

He chuckled. "I take it you got what you wanted."

She hugged him tightly.

"I'm not sure I'll ever get what I want, but at least I'll get what I need, and that's closure." She considered her situation and what it had done to her. Humiliation was like a pervasive, hungry disease. It was like a cancer that ate her up from the inside out. It nibbled at her self-esteem and gnawed at her confidence. What they had done to her was a swift character assassination. A sniper that ended it all with one stupid hit.

"What happens now?"

She smiled. "We go to Maisey's and have lunch, and then we wait." She lifted on tiptoes and kissed him gently but sensually. Something felt different about the kiss. Somehow it felt more rewarding, and maybe it was because she initiated it. When she pulled back, she saw the look of concern on his face. "What?" she asked.

He shook his head. "Nothing." Beads of sweat gathered on his brow.

"Are you nervous about the film crew?"

He stepped back. "No. I mean, why should I be. I'm not the one on camera."

She laughed. "You must not have heard. You're my new sidekick, and I've negotiated a decent salary for you too, but if it's not enough, you can tell them."

His head snapped back. "I know nothing about construction or performing for an audience. I only do what you tell me to do."

"Which makes you the perfect partner. This isn't a circus." She laughed. "Well, it kind of is, but you're not part of that dog and pony show. I am the ringmaster, and you're... I don't know who you are, but at least you'll get paid for it."

"Is me following directions the only thing that makes me a perfect partner?"

She loved the way his eyes sparkled when he smiled, just like they were now. "No, you're not an asshole. You won't use me to serve your purposes, and I can trust you. Besides, you're not a bad kisser." For a moment, she thought he might be sick with the way his skin turned white and appeared clammy. "You okay?"

He nodded and rubbed his stomach. "How about that blue plate special at Maisey's, my treat?"

As they climbed into his car, she took a notepad from her purse and started on a new list.

*50 Ways to happiness*
*Trust the right people*
*Wear underwear that fit*
*Never mix beer with hard alcohol*
*Live life on my terms*
*Kiss the right man*

She drew three stars next to that. As she looked at Mason's profile, she smiled. He wasn't her type, but somehow that made him perfect, and he made her happy.

She arrived at Maisey's with a spring in her step and a smile on her face and breezed through the door, but Mason halted. She glanced to see what stopped him and saw him look toward a table where Wes and Lydia Covington sat eating burgers.

The only place open was the booth beside them, so she rushed to grab it.

"Come on. I'm starving."

Mason shoved his hands in his pockets and dragged his feet to the booth.

"Mason," Wes nodded as he said the name, but

he didn't smile, and she wondered what was up between the two.

"That's right, you two know each other."

"Yep, we grew up together."

"Here, in Aspen Cove?"

Wes shook his head. "No, in Denver, but we spent summers here until ..."

Mason groaned.

"Until what?" she asked.

Wes wiped his mouth and set his napkin down. "Until his family screwed mine over."

"Listen," Mason said with an earnest voice. "That was then, but this is now. That deal wasn't me, and I regret not speaking up, but hell man, you know how my family is."

Wes took his wallet out of his pocket. "I do, and I know the apple doesn't fall far from the tree. We never think we're like our parents, and then you hear yourself speak, and you say, 'hell, I sound like my dad.'" He took two twenties from his wallet and put them on the table. "Look, it's water under the bridge." He turned to Jewel. "Just be careful. That D in their middle name isn't really for der. It's deceitful or downright dirty. The Van der Veens will do whatever it takes to make a sale."

Mason's shoulders dropped and rolled forward. "I'm not my father."

Wes bent over and kissed Lydia on the cheek. "I'll see you at home, sweetheart."

Once Wes left, Lydia turned to face Mason. "Care to shed some light on what just happened?"

"It's a Hatfield and McCoy story. Our parents had a falling out, and we got banned from seeing each other."

"That doesn't sound like Wes," she said. "He's not a grudge holder."

"Well, there was a multimillion-dollar deal that went sideways because my father took advantage of a gentleman's agreement. That deal nearly put the Covington's out of business. I could've said something in court, but I didn't. I was afraid of what my father might do."

"Oh," Lydia squeaked. "You're the splinter in Wes's side then—the one who owns all the other properties in town."

"More like a jagged plank that has caused an old wound to fester. He was my best friend, but I chose family over friendship. If I had to do it all again, I'd choose differently."

"Maybe you should tell him that," Lydia said.

"I should, and I will." He rose from his seat. "Let me see if I can catch him."

When Mason was gone, Lydia moved to the space across from Jewel. "Lots of excitement happening on your side of town."

"I take it you know who I am too."

Lydia laughed. "Everyone has been whispering about it for months."

"Why didn't anyone say anything?"

"We respect people's wishes. If you weren't flaunting it, then we weren't bringing it up. You're not the first celebrity to hide out here. They had Samantha before you. I'm fairly certain you won't be the last."

"I love this town." She loved the way the people protected each other. Living in Aspen Cove was like living in the arms of a giant hug.

"I love it too, but it took me some time to get from loathing to love. I came here looking for something different. I wanted a big clinic, an important job, lots of money, and validation. What I wanted and what I needed were two different things. It took almost losing everything to realize what I had. Aspen Cove isn't bright lights and big things, but I've learned over time that it's the small things that truly matter. It's not what you get from others but what you give that fills you up. I was empty until the town showed me what full felt like. I'll never leave this town." Lydia stood. "Blue plate is a green chili burger today. I highly recommend it if you like spicy food." She smiled. "Now that you know we know, I can finally say, welcome to Aspen Cove JJ Monroe."

"It's Jewel, and I'm happy to be here."

As she sat alone, considering her life, she realized that she could've stopped anywhere for a snack, but the universe led her to Aspen Cove and straight into a small-town grocery store that needed a new owner. Was that fate or pure luck?

"What'll it be?" Maisey asked as she swept over, dangling the coffee pot between two fingers.

"Blue plate special times two."

She looked at the empty seat across from her. "You got a date?"

"Yes, I think I might if he ever comes back."

"Two blue plates coming up, and if that man doesn't show, he's an idiot." Maisey pivoted, and the squeak of her white loafers faded as she neared the kitchen.

Jewel took out her list and added a few more lines.

- Blue plate specials
- A community that cares
- A man who values who you are and not what you offer

Thinking about men and dates made her consider Mason. Was he "the one" or simply the next one to break her heart?

# CHAPTER EIGHTEEN

He chased Wes down to the big Victorian on Rose Lane—the house where he'd spent a lot of his youth.

"Hey, man, can we talk?" He shut the door to his SUV and walked toward Wes, who leaned against his truck.

"Not much to say." Wes crossed his arms over his chest and scowled.

"You bought your gran's place. I always loved this house."

"It has lots of wonderful memories and a few bad."

Mason would've sworn the temp dropped ten degrees at the end of that sentence.

"I want to make things right."

Wes kicked off his truck and started toward the door. "You can't, but honestly, I'm over it."

"If that's true, then can we be friends again?" He missed the time he spent with Wes. He was the sibling Mason wished he had. Instead, he got a sister who was as annoying as a mosquito in summer, even at thirtysomething.

"I understand why you did what you did—actually, why you did nothing. And I can't fault you because family is family." He rubbed at his finely trimmed beard, his hand making a sandpaper sound against his face. "I had to choose a few years ago to stick with the status quo or forge my path. I chose to count on me."

Mason hoped to choose a similar route, but with the jump start of thirty-five million dollars.

"Good on you. I'm tying up some loose ends, and then I'll be figuring out what I want to do for the rest of my life. Working for Elite isn't it."

Wes nodded. "Are you and Jewel a thing?"

He didn't know how to answer that. They were something, but he couldn't say what. "We're testing the waters."

Wes gave him the exact look Heidi used to give him when he got caught doing something bad. "Whatever you do, don't mess with her. She's a resident of this town, and we take care of our own."

"I'm a resident of this town too, so does the same consideration and care apply to me?"

Wes chuckled. "You're temporary; she's got her heels dug in with a house and a business. What do you have here?"

*Not a damn thing.*

"Gotcha. Don't worry. My intentions are good."

"What's happening with the news crew camped at your place?" Wes asked.

Mason let out a groan. "That was my father at work. I think he did it to sabotage me. He thought telling the press that she was in town to ruin another house would make it harder to sell the one we are refurbishing, but it did the opposite. It let her old show *Reno or Wreck It* know where to find her, and they offered her a deal."

Wes's brows lifted high enough to disappear under his fringe of bangs.

"She's going back to the show?"

It wasn't quite that simple. "No, they're coming here. She gets airtime to prove she's good at what she does and who she is. The show gets another chance at ratings."

"What do you get? I've never known a Van der Veen to enter a deal and not have the lion's share of the benefits."

There was no point in arguing, but the truth didn't make him feel less dirty. He'd made a back-alley deal not only to sell his house for a significant profit, but he'd be able to dump the remaining houses and gain his trust fund and possibly his father's respect.

"I get the house remodeled and a guaranteed sale."

"That's a sweet deal."

"It is." He offered his hand for a shake. "Can we call it a truce? Once this whole thing blows over with the house, can we grab a beer?"

Wes smiled. "I'd like that." He looked toward town. "Don't you have a lunch date?"

"Oh shit. I left and didn't consider her." He felt awful and hoped that Jewel wasn't waiting for him to order lunch.

"Don't make that a habit. When you find a good thing, you need to treat her right and put her needs before everything."

"When did you become so wise?"

Wes chuckled. "When I met Lydia, but she tells me I'm still in training." He opened the door, and a giant German shepherd charged at him.

Mason froze, thinking the dog was about to attack.

"That's Sarge, he's a retired police dog, and while he could probably rip your arm off, he'll most likely lick you to death."

He ruffled the dog's fur before climbing back into his car and returning to the diner.

He found Jewel at the same booth, sitting at a table with two blue-plate specials. Hers was halfway finished.

"Sorry about that." He slid onto the red bench across from her. "I needed to mend some fences."

"Did you?" She forked a bit of hamburger drowned in green chili and stuck it in her mouth. "This is amazing," she garbled out.

He scooped a bite onto his fork and tasted it. He didn't like super spicy foods, but the chili had just enough of a kick to make his tongue tingle but not require an ice water chaser.

"It is good." He glanced down at her list. "What's on today's list? Should I warn anyone of impending doom?"

She shifted the page to face him, and he read her scribbled entries. They made his heart feel heavy, because deep down inside, he knew he owed her the truth. He had manipulated her into the deal by pointing out the upside. He never told her he would benefit from it as well. He'd signed her on to six houses, and she didn't even know it yet.

"What's this *Kiss the right man* entry?" He pointed to the bullet point next to it. "Have you found him yet?" It was easier to focus on that than the one that said, *A man who values who you are and not what you offer,* or the one above it that said, *Trust the right people.*

"I don't know. He's kissed me a few times, and they were pretty great. I'd love to check out his other skill sets."

Mason choked on his next bite. "Is this an interview? You want references, or is it a trial offer?"

She swirled the melted cheese through the chili. "You are a good snuggler."

"I am, and I guarantee that's not where my talents end."

She wiggled in her seat and rounded her lips into an O shape to let out an oooh sound. "Are you flirting with me?"

He pointed to himself. "Me? You're the one talking about skill sets and kisses. I'm all for the on-the-job interview."

"Hmm." she dropped her fork and rubbed her chin. "I think we can arrange that. Just promise me you won't turn out to be another Matt. I don't know what I'd do if I gave my heart and body to a man who didn't deserve it."

Talk about a hit to the chest. Those words were like a wrecking ball slamming into his sternum. He needed to come clean and tell her what he'd done. Just as he opened his mouth to talk, Sylvia and Matt walked in.

"Speak of the devil." Jewel leaned in and whispered. "The problem is, I'm not sure which of them is worse."

He wanted to raise his hand and scream, it's me—I'm worse.

"I got all the paperwork together on our way back here. It's the standard contract. The one you signed when you started." Sylvia nudged Jewel over and sat beside her, leaving Matt awkwardly standing at the end of the table.

"Pull up a chair," Sylvia said, pointing to the empty seat at a nearby table.

Matt did as he was told. He seemed like a guy who'd had his manhood cut off, and by the looks of it, Sylvia was wearing it.

"As you requested, there's the ten percent raise you asked for." She took a pen, pointed out the changes, and then laid the pen where Jewel was supposed to sign.

Before she could, Mason reached for the pen. "Shouldn't you read the whole thing first?"

Jewel laughed. "It's a standard contract. I've seen it before, and it doesn't look any different this time." She picked up the pen and made the J of her name before he stopped her again.

"But what about the fine print? Shouldn't you have a lawyer look over it?"

"Geez, Mason, it's not like we're asking her to sign her organs over; it's a standard contract."

Jewel finished signing her name, and he felt like he'd just sent her to slaughter. He had to remind himself that it was a win-win situation. Actually, a win-win-win-win if he counted all four of them. If he kept telling himself that, he might just believe it.

Jewel would get her closure, he'd get his trust fund, and Sylvia and Matt would keep their paychecks. Yes, it was a win all around.

"You're looking pale again," Jewel said. "Are you sure you're okay?"

He gulped his glass of water and set it down. "Yep, I think I waited too long to eat is all."

Jewel looked at her phone. "I think I'm going to check on Beth and put the order in at the store."

Matt narrowed his eyes. "The store? You own the store here."

Jewel smiled. "Yes, there is life after you."

"But how are you going to do that and—"

Sylvia pushed out of the booth, knocking over the rest of Mason's water into Matt's lap.

"Holy hell," Matt grabbed a napkin to mop up the water.

"That's my cue to exit," Jewel said. "Tell the crew to be ready by eight. This shouldn't take more than a week or two tops."

Mason watched as a frustrated Matt opened his mouth to speak, but Sylvia's dirty look silenced him.

"Eight it is. I'll get Mason's contract set, and we'll

begin. See you tomorrow." As Jewel turned to walk away, Sylvia stopped her. "Is there a place nearby where we can get a room?" She looked at Matt. "Two rooms actually and lodging for the crew?"

"We have one bed-and-breakfast. You're better off trying Copper Creek."

Sylvia pouted. "But that's so far away."

Jewel shrugged. "Beggars can't be choosers."

Mason knew it was a jab at the producer because she had begged Jewel for her help.

As soon as Jewel exited the diner, Sylvia took her seat.

"What the hell are you doing? If I didn't know better, I'd say you were trying to stop her from signing the contract."

He shook his head. "No, I'm just making sure she knows what she's getting into."

She pulled another set of papers from her bag. "This is your contract. It says that we'll refurb the house and buy it. It also states that we'll do the same with the remaining properties Elite owns in Aspen Cove provided Jewel fulfills her contract."

"What if she doesn't?" There was a good chance she wouldn't have signed if she'd looked at the fine print. He rubbed his face, and his stomach did a triple somersault and threatened to lose what little he'd eaten.

"Then she's in breach of contract."

"And what does that mean?"

"She could be liable for whatever the show loses."

"She doesn't have anything for you to take if she won't do it. Look, you two have already taken everything from her."

Matt chuckled. "She has a store, and she owns the house you two are shacking up in, right?"

Mason swallowed the bile rising in his throat. No matter what, he'd make sure Jewel wouldn't lose anything. Even if she refused to do the other episodes, by then, he'd have his money, and he'd buy back everything she lost. Inside his head, he heard his conscience speak ... *What about her self-respect, ego, and trust? Can I buy those back?*

# CHAPTER NINETEEN

"Hey Jewel," Beth said as Jewel walked inside the store. "How's the house coming along?"

She scrubbed her face with her hands and let them drop to her sides. Her right hitting her bag with the contracts in it.

She rounded the corner to the register and saw the veritable smorgasbord set out in front of Beth. Lined up like sacrifices at the altar were a bag of Fritos, a Hershey bar, a granola snack, and a vacuum-packed pickle.

"Getting more cravings, huh?" She glanced down at Beth's bump and wondered how much was junk food and how much was the baby?

"Oh, it's a salty-sweet thing—I've got the sweets bookended with salty goodness." She pointed to the

Fritos, then the pickle. "The problem is, once I finish the cycle, it starts all over again. Too bad there isn't a perfect sweet and salty snack. You know, an all-in-one treat." She slid her hands over her growing belly. "If I keep this up, I'll be as big as an elephant before I give birth."

A random piece of trivia entered her mind. "Elephants are pregnant for close to two years."

"Can you imagine? I'd be as big as this house." She looked behind her. "Speaking of houses."

Jewel held up a hand. "Yes, there is a crew on their way to film the remaining renovation of the Hyacinth house."

Beth's eyes grew wide. "You got your job back?"

It was a long story, and she was too tired to go into it. "I'm doing a friend a favor." In her mind, that's how she justified letting the crew in to record the work. To admit it was about her sounded egotistical. If she told herself it was about helping Mason get his trust, then it seemed more altruistic.

That was the same line of thinking when she said she'd help him with the other house, but the truth was he gave her a smoking deal on her property, and she had an itch to build that needed scratching. Her little redo of the Corner Store stoked her creative fires and made her want a bigger project, but she couldn't afford one. Everyone thinks that you're rich because you're on TV, but that simply wasn't true.

She and Matt hadn't climbed the ladder to sit on the top rung with *The Property Brothers* or the *Fixer Upper* couple, but they had been rising fast. Jewel closed her eyes and wondered what her life would've looked like if she'd chosen a better man.

"Earth to Jewel."

She shook her head and stared at Beth.

"Sorry, I went someplace else for a minute."

Beth laughed. "I have a cognitive vacation every once in a while too. Anyway, I wasn't talking about the film crew. I was hoping you could check out your place. It smells like something died up there."

"What?"

Beth lifted her nose into the air. "Can't you smell it? It's like musty old laundry."

"Oh my God." She'd only been back in her place to pick up clothes. For all intents and purposes, she'd packed up and shacked up with Mason. "I'm so sorry."

She bolted for the stairs and took them two at a time to the top, where the smell of mold got stronger. When she opened the door, she saw green, literally. A sense of relief and fear rushed through her at the same time. She was grateful it wasn't black mold, but that didn't mean it wasn't lurking below the flooring.

"Stupid," she chastised herself. Without another thought, she opened the windows that covered one wall and started ripping up the floor. It wasn't a difficult task given the space was less than a thousand square feet, and whatever adhesive they'd used was soft from water damage.

"What's going on up there?" Beth called from below.

"Damage control."

"Carry on then."

Jewel spent the next two hours hauling flooring out of the space and setting up fans. When she made it back downstairs, Beth was working on her next round of snacks. This time the sacrifices were a bag of Bugles, a Little Debbie Nutty Bar, and a package of salted nuts. Beth was right; she'd be big in no time if she didn't get the cravings under control.

"I know. I'm out of control, and I pay for this." She rolled her eyes. "Well, not the Fritos because they were part of my compensation package, but I buy the rest."

Jewel laughed. "I'm not worried about the cost of snacks."

"You should be. I could eat you into a whole new bracket of deliveries. Even the chip guy commented about our increased inventory numbers."

"Try this." Jewel walked down the candy aisle to get a PAYDAY Bar. "It's salty and sweet. Another thing you might want to add to the order is chocolate-covered pretzels. They might fit the bill too." She swiped a bag of trail mix from the stand on her way back. "These should work as well."

Beth eyed the offerings. She didn't look convinced but opened the PAYDAY Bar and took a bite. As soon as the big smile flashed across her face, Jewel knew she'd done her job.

"Do you need me to do anything before I leave?"

Beth shook her head but never stopped chewing the nougat snack. "Nope," she said after a swallow. "I've got next week's order ready."

How lucky was Jewel to have hired the perfect woman to man her store? Beth was organized and dependable and precisely what Jewel needed. The store hadn't been this put together since she bought it. While Jewel liked to think it was because she'd remodeled it with efficiency in mind, she knew Beth was the one who kept it running smoothly after her abrupt departure.

She hadn't missed working at the store at all because she was in her happy place. Give her a hammer and nails and a room to refurbish, and she was in heaven.

"Sorry about the smell. I didn't consider the mold, but it's not dangerous to you."

Beth's hand went to her stomach. "I never thought about that."

"You're probably in more danger eating that shit." She pointed to the row of snacks. "But it will take a day to air out. Crank up the heat in here if you want because I've got the windows open upstairs."

"It's supposed to snow again."

Jewel let out a breath that sounded like a horse's snort. "I'll be back to close things up before it gets too bad."

"Okay, don't forget."

"I never forget." She grabbed her bag and walked toward the door.

"Says the woman with a mold problem."

Jewel shook her head. "You're right. I was distracted." She turned to see Beth tap her chin.

"Hunky real estate mogul, house renovation, new home, and now a film crew. I'd say your mind is busy."

"I'd say you're right." She walked out of the store with thoughts of how her life had taken a turn in the last few days. She'd run from her marriage and the embarrassment of her failure. And it was her failure. While she didn't finance the show, she ran it, and any captain goes down with the ship, even if it was a sailor that poked a hole in the boat. It was easier to blame others than take responsibility.

She climbed into her SUV and headed home. That had a sweet ring to it. Even without the remodel, her small house on Hyacinth had become home, and it had nothing to do with the house but the occupant. She hated to admit it, but she was falling hard for Mason. He was hunky and sweet and frustrating all at the same time. That morning, she wanted to throttle him, but tonight she wanted to hug him.

He talked her into doing the show, and she felt good about it. It was her show, her way. This time she would not let anyone take advantage of her. No one would pull the wool over her eyes.

She parked in the driveway and was happy to see that only one news crew remained.

Feeling generous and in good spirits, she waved and called out hello.

"Can I ask a few questions," the male reporter called from where he leaned against the side of his car.

"Sure. Happy to answer anything." It was funny how perspective changed everything. It was kind of like being a caged animal. When locked inside, she felt vulnerable and the need to be on guard constantly. By agreeing to do the show, she opened the lock to her pen, and she felt free and non-threatened.

"How do you feel about working with your ex-husband?" He pulled his notepad from his pocket and jotted down something.

"It's fine. I don't look at him and see my ex-husband. He's a coworker. There is no emotional attachment between us."

"You don't think there'll be any hard feelings?"

He chuckled. "I was kind of looking forward to the fireworks, hammers flying, a two-by-four to the side of the head thing."

She imagined her list and smiled. "More like a nail gun accident, but no. We are both professionals." Even as she said it, it felt false. If Matt were indeed a professional, he would've put the house and the crew's safety first, but he didn't because he was only thinking about his nail gun. "It's one show and a short one at that. The kitchen and living room are complete, so it's a bath and bedroom show."

"Bedroom, huh?" He smiled, and his bushy mustache followed. If Jewel didn't know better, she would've thought he was a relative of Geraldo Rivera.

"There is nothing but construction happening in those bedrooms."

He stared at her for a moment like he didn't believe her. "What about you and Mason Van der Veen?"

"What about us?" Was there an us to that equation? They'd kissed plenty of times but hadn't moved past that. They slept together, but that was all that happened ... sleep. She internally shook her head. That wasn't entirely true. She had a habit of seeking him out in the night and snuggling into him like he was her heater. There were days when she'd wake up with the blankets tossed aside, and all that covered her were Mason's arms. She loved those days—the days when their limbs were so tangled there was no beginning to her or ending for him.

"Are you two ... a thing?"

She laughed. "We are a lot of things, but a couple isn't one of them." She could say that with certainty because there had been no discussion of what they were together. Separately, she was a scorned woman intent on setting the record straight, and he was a neglected child still trying to win his father's approval and get his trust fund.

"Which house will be next?"

That was a simple question to answer. "Mine," she said with a smile before walking away.

When she entered her house, the scent of Mason's famous garlic chicken and mashed potatoes floated through the air.

"Honey, I'm home," she called out.

He peeked his head around the kitchen door. "I wondered if you'd ever come home and join me for a celebratory dinner."

She took in his messy hair and the kitchen towel draped over his shoulder. He was a good-looking man. Who wouldn't fall for a guy who could cook? Add in that he was nice, confident, and well-dressed unless he wore his driving moccasins, and you had a recipe for attraction. He wasn't pushy and didn't have an agenda except for the one she knew. That honesty drew her to him. He'd been nothing but forthright with his intentions and desires. He even warned her before their first kiss. Yep, Mason Van der Veen was a good man.

"I'd love to celebrate. Do we have wine?"

He rushed into the kitchen and came back with a bottle of Pinot Grigio. "We're all set. Dinner will be ready in about fifteen minutes if you want to change or shower or whatever."

She moved toward him with one thought on her mind, and that was tasting his lips. A meal was always better with an appetizer.

"I'm going to kiss you," she warned before wrapping her hand around his neck and pulling him down so she could reach his lips.

The kiss was gentle and romantic at first. He tasted like her future, which was sweet and satisfying.

Soft lips melded together, tongues delicately dancing, and their hands reaching and groping for fistfuls of whatever they could capture. He cupped her bottom, whereas all she got was her fingers in his hair. Her grip on him kept Mason right where she wanted him—fused to her body.

He pulled back and sucked in a breath. "Wow, that was—"

"Delicious," she finished for him. "I think I'll take a shower and change into something more comfortable." Any other time that might mean lingerie or something sexy, but all she had was flannel pajamas and her fuzzy gray slippers. Somehow, she didn't think it mattered what she wore. Mason never complained. Yep, he was perfect. As she walked to the bedroom, her inner self reminded her that no one was perfect.

"True," she said out loud, "But he's as close as I'll ever get." With that thought, she started the shower and decided that tonight, she'd start something else with Mason. After that kiss in the kitchen, there wasn't a doubt where they'd be going next. She couldn't wait to climb between his fancy sheets and level up their relationship.

# CHAPTER TWENTY

What the hell was he supposed to do. His body was vibrating with need, but his head was pounding from stress. While he never intended to do Jewel wrong, he couldn't help but think he did.

He plated the chicken and opened the wine. He had this whole celebratory dinner planned with wine and candles, but was it wise to take her there before he came clean? She was getting roped into a situation because of him and his ego and his greed.

Every time he considered the thirty-five million, he justified his actions because that kind of money could fix about anything. Hell, he could buy her a production company, and she could start her own show.

"That smells amazing." She breezed past him

and took a seat at the table. Her floral scent wrapped him in a sensory hug.

"I hope you enjoy it."

"Feels like a celebration and the last meal before I walk the green mile to my execution."

His heart dropped into his stomach, or maybe it was his stomach that hit the floor. He didn't know, but it didn't feel good.

"Are you regretting your decision?"

To say it was her decision was pushing it. He grew up with one of the best manipulators in the business and had learned a thing or two about taking an idea and making someone else think it's theirs. Selling houses was like selling used cars, only there was a heftier price tag.

"No, I'm just feeling nervous and nostalgic. Hindsight is always 20/20, and what was will always seem better than what is. I don't want to set myself up for a big disappointment if things go to hell on day one."

"Why would they?" Nervous energy twisted his stomach.

"I talked to a reporter outside."

He swallowed the acid in his throat. Had the reporter seen the contract? "What did he or she say?" Maybe he wouldn't have to out himself. Perhaps the press had already done it. He took in her demeanor and the look on her face. Nothing said. I'm *pissed and feel betrayed.* If anything, she looked calm but cautious.

"He asked how I felt about working with my ex, and I feel okay about it, but I'm coming from a place of where we used to be. He's not. The show has been his for almost a year, which means he's the one calling the shots. It's not really how I feel about working with him. It's how he'll feel about working with me."

Mason let out a sigh. "I'm sure he feels relieved. You're saving the day for them. He's probably happy to step aside and let you take the reins. If he could do it himself, they wouldn't have come begging you to step back into your role."

"You're right, but something feels off. He's too amendable."

"Desperation makes people do things they wouldn't think to do normally."

"True." She giggled. "I never saw myself living in small-town Colorado, owning a grocery store and a rundown house."

He swallowed hard. If she didn't fulfill her end of the contract, she might not even have that.

"But here you are."

"Yes, here I am," she picked up her glass of wine and held it in the air. "Let's toast to a bigger, brighter future and all the good things yet to come."

She looked like she was going to eat him up instead of the chicken. There was a fiery passion in her eyes that went with the kiss she gave him earlier.

He knew he had to set things straight. Otherwise, he wouldn't be able to live with himself. Van der Veen blood might run through his veins, but it was Heidi's voice that ran through his head. *Always treat a woman with respect. Be honest. Be faithful. Give more than you take. Love her with everything you have.*

"About the contract..."

Jewel waved her hand through the air. "No more talk about the show or the contract or my ex. Let's enjoy this amazing dinner you fixed, and we can celebrate us. We're an unlikely pair, but somehow it works."

"Are we a pair?"

She blushed. "I didn't mean that you and I were a thing. Only that despite our differences and your complete and utter lack of construction talent, we work well together." She sipped her wine and lowered her head while her cheeks glowed red.

While it would be better to get things over and out in the open, he understood her need for a night of calm before what would be weeks of chaos.

She cut a piece of chicken and took a bite.

"I swear this gets better each time you make it."

He chuckled. "I've only made it once before."

She brightened the room with her smile. "I know,

but it's better this time. Maybe you had a case of nerves the first time." She scooped up a bite of mashed potatoes and put them in her mouth. While she moved them around and swallowed, her cheeks turned brighter red. "Kind of like the first time you have sex with someone. Don't you ever get performance anxiety?"

She reached for her glass of wine and gulped it down.

Immediately, he reached for the bottle to fill her glass up.

"I'm confident I could please."

She stabbed another bite. "If you make love the way you kiss, I'm confident too. Are you a passionate lover, Mason?"

Was she making a pass at him? It's not as if his mind didn't go there all the time. He was convinced the studies were right, and men thought about sex every seven seconds because he did. But not just sex; he thought about it with her. Never in his life would he have thought steel-toed boots were sexy, but inside hers were pink painted toenails. Torn jeans always had their appeal, but hers fit her bottom like a glove, and he envisioned his hand in that glove squeezing her cheeks. Then there were the power tools. Thinking about how she mastered them made his jeans uncomfortably tight.

He cleared his mind and his throat.

"I haven't had many complaints."

She nearly choked on her bite of potatoes. "Not many? That means your admitting to a few."

He took his time chewing. He liked the way she focused her attention on him, especially his mouth, and figured he'd play along. When he swallowed, he licked his lips and then took a sip of wine, letting a drop glisten on his lower lip before his tongue swept out to catch it. He made love to her with his eyes while she squirmed in her seat.

"The complaints are never about the quality, just the quantity." He knew that came out wrong.

She smiled. "Lacking in that department?" She puckered her lips and made a pouty, frowning face. "You know. It's not what you have but what you do with it." She sat up. "I once read a book called *The Dean's List* where this guy had a small you know what. She called it a button." Her hand waved through the air as if to dismiss the subject. "Anyway, the guy had to compensate for his lack of ..." she shrugged. "You get what I mean. So, the girl he was with taught him oral skills by showing him how to eat peaches."

It was his turn to choke on his food. Once he stopped, he asked. "Peaches? How does one learn from eating peaches?"

She ate her last bite of chicken and set her plate aside. "I'll get you the book."

He finished his dinner and tried to explain himself. "No complaints in either of those areas. I was simply trying to say that while I'm blessed in all things." He felt the heat of a blush rising to his cheeks. "Most women want more of what I offer."

Her lips twisted, then curled into a smile. "So, it's staying power that's your problem."

She seemed to enjoy this immensely, and even though his sexual ability was under scrutiny, he was reveling in the banter.

"I refuse to answer another question about my sexual prowess fearing you'll turn it around, and before I know it, you'll have me convinced I have a vagina."

"Now, wouldn't that be interesting?"

"Shocking more like it."

"For both of us," she said and rose from her seat, picking up their plates.

"I'll get that. You go find a movie and relax."

She set the dishes in the sink and pointed to the living room.

"You cooked, so I'll clean. You can even pick the movie, but if you make me watch another *Terminator*, I'll hurt you."

"Do you have a list of ways to kill me off too?"

"Not yet, but that can be arranged. You know how I love my lists."

He chuckled all the way to the sofa, where he

took his spot on the right side and turned on HGTV. Most women would swoon at *Sixteen Candles* or *Love Actually,* but not his Jewel. *His Jewel?* He was in real trouble with this woman. He was like a teenager experiencing his first crush.

She came in just as *Brother vs. Brother* started. Instead of sitting on her side of the couch, she sat next to him and drew her legs up, tucking them under her bottom, forcing her to lean his way.

In any other situation, he'd jump all over the gesture. There was no doubt in his mind that Jewel wanted to move things to the next level, but he couldn't think about that until he told her everything. He refused to take another thing from her.

He raised his hands in the air and stretched. "I think I'm going to hit the bed. We have a big day ahead of us, and I want to be rested." Before she could convince him to stay, he stood, and she toppled into his empty spot.

"But it's early."

She was right. The last time he'd been to bed this early was when he was five, and it wasn't his idea.

"I know, but I'm exhausted." He bent over and kissed her forehead. "Snuggle up when you come to bed." He knew she would because she was metal, and he was a magnet. For whatever reason, she always sought him out in her sleep. If she didn't, he'd find her. She was the moon, and he the tide. She the honey and he the bee. She was the light and him the moth. It was inevitable—they were drawn together.

As he got ready for bed and slipped between the sheets, he wondered if he could salvage what they'd started. Or would their relationship be another failure? Only this time, would he be able to wheel and deal his way out of it, or would he end up emotionally bankrupt too?

# CHAPTER TWENTY-ONE

It was only noon, and Jewel wanted to quit. Matt was an idiot, but it just brought back memories of the time before when he acted the fool. He refused to follow directions and treated Mason like a servant.

They finished the demo of both bathrooms, and because Matt was such an inconsiderate prick, Jewel put the nicest tile she could in the bathrooms. There was no reason to budget and skimp. This would be the only project she would work on, so Sylvia couldn't take it from the budget of the next house. And since they agreed to buy the house from Mason, there was no loss that he would have to absorb from the extravagant marble flooring and tub surround she'd ordered that morning for delivery that afternoon.

"Clean this up," Matt snapped at Mason.

Jewel was at her breaking point. Matt was acting the king, and she was sure if Mason had a fiddle, Matt would have him play a song right after he fetched him his slippers and a glass of wine.

"Stop it." She fisted her hips and stomped her foot. "He isn't yours to boss around."

Matt narrowed his eyes at her. "I can do whatever I want. This is my—"

"Your what?" She lifted a brow and waited for him to say, "my show." She begged the universe to let those words slip from his mouth, but he caught himself and snapped his lips closed. "I didn't think so." She turned to Mason. "You want to have lunch?"

"Lunch sounds amazing," Matt said. "Shall we go to the diner? I think that Maisey woman has the hots for me."

"Maisey is happily married."

Matt chuckled. "That's what they all say."

"If you want to go to Maisey's, you are on your own." She slid her arm through Mason's and walked toward the door. "We have a date."

"We do?" Mason said.

"Yes, you owe me since you abandoned me last night." She hated to be so direct, but that's what it felt like. Things got a little steamy, and he ran.

He pushed the door open and followed her outside.

"I didn't abandon you. I was tired."

He walked her to his car and helped her into the passenger seat. Before he could close the door, Sylvia ran out of the house.

"Where are you going?"

Jewel looked at the clock on her phone. "It's lunchtime, and we're hungry."

Sylvia pressed her lips together. "But we always ate as a crew."

Jewel shook her head. "That was before you slept with my husband. I don't know what you think this is, but we aren't friends. We can be friendly, but that's as far as I'll go."

Sylvia narrowed her eyes. "We'll have to figure out how to make it work—how to find our way back to a place where we can both be happy since we'll be working together for the foreseeable future."

Jewel closed the door. "Let's go."

"You okay?"

She turned in her seat to face him. The belt tugged at her shoulder. "I forgot what an asshole he was, and I'm sorry. He's making you pay for all the anger he feels toward me."

"He's angry at you?"

"Sure, I don't think he ever thought I'd file for divorce. I imagine he expected me to put up with his infidelity."

"He's an idiot."

"We agree on that. I don't know why she wants to be friends. In a couple of weeks, this show will be over, and they'll be gone. It just makes little sense."

Mason gripped the wheel until his knuckles turned white.

She reached over and rubbed her hand on his arm. "I know it's stressful for you. He's treating you like an indentured servant. Somehow it's like he's doing you a favor when in reality, it's you doing him one by letting them film on location at your house. A million things could go wrong." She chuckled. "Like a load-bearing wall that buckles."

He pulled onto Main Street and into the nearest parking spot. "I have it on good authority that the wall in the kitchen wasn't load-bearing."

"You had it inspected, and because of my experience, I had Wes double-check it before we tore it down."

"Wes was in the house?"

She smiled. "Yes, and I didn't tell you because I got the feeling there was something amiss between you too, and after the showdown at Maisey's, I was right to hold that information back."

"You're a sneaky one."

"I try to be honest in all things, but there are moments when it's important to hold your cards close to your chest. You never want to show your hand completely. Where is the fun in that?"

Tension stiffened his shoulders. "Honesty is important." He frowned, and she wanted to yank him over to her side of the car and hug him.

"Hey, whatever is bothering you, let it go. Let's eat and have a work-free lunch, and then we'll go back and see the tile I ordered. It's amazing and so far out of our original budget."

"You stuck it to them with the tile?"

She exited and waited for him on the curb.

"Sticking it to them wasn't the intent, but making sure the purchaser got an amazing house is important to me. While the porcelain tile was fine, the Carrera marble will be amazing and will show well on film."

"You got Carrera marble?"

"I did." She grinned

He opened the door to Maisey's, and they found a booth next to Doc's.

"Hey, Doc," Jewel said.

He lowered his paper and grumbled something about being nice until he had two cups of coffee, then raised his paper again.

"Man of few words?"

She laughed. "Oh, no. He's a regular chatterbox and the voice of wisdom in town."

The paper came down. "You want some wisdom? Get rid of the mold smell in your apartment, and your neighbors might like you more."

"I took care of it yesterday."

Mason watched the banter. "You had mold?"

She wanted to roll her eyes but didn't because that was rude.

"It wasn't the dangerous mold. More like a musty smell coming from under the flooring where the water seeped and stayed stagnant." Her hand went to her mouth. "Oh no, I left the window open, and it snowed some last night." She rose from the booth. "Order the blue plate for me. I'll be right back." She bolted out the door and down the street to her store.

When she entered, Beth was behind the counter eating a PAYDAY Bar. She whizzed past her and up the stairs. At the top, she stopped and took a bracing breath. It hadn't snowed a lot, but a few inches. Hopefully, she didn't walk into a disaster area.

She closed her eyes and turned the knob, throwing the door open like it was some kind of big reveal. What she saw brought a sense of relief. The room was cold, but only a dusting of snow was on the floor, and since she'd already pulled it up, nothing was damaged.

She closed the windows, cleaned up the snow, and headed back downstairs.

"Everything good?" Beth asked.

"Yep."

"You forgot, didn't you? "

"Yep."

"Do I need to do anything?"

She shook her head. "Nope."

"Can I trade my Fritos compensation in for PAYDAY Bars?"

Jewel laughed. "You can have anything you want."

"Oh, good, because I ate a box of Raspberry Zingers."

Jewel gasped. "Those are Mason's."

"Should I order more? I have to say, they are amazing."

Jewel's stomach grumbled. "I'm starving."

Beth offered her a PAYDAY Bar. "No thanks, I've got a blue plate special waiting for me."

"Oooh," Beth's eyes opened like a hawk seeking prey. "What is it today?"

Jewel had no idea. "Does it matter? Everything they make is good and guaranteed to clog your arteries, but you'll leave happy."

"Until the heart attack."

"True, but Doc is nearby, so there's that." She started for the door. "You want me to bring you back something?"

"No, Gray is cooking tonight."

"He cooks?" She smiled. "Mason cooks too. Like Julia Child type of cooking."

"Lucky girl, Gray is more of a take-and-bake guy, but he tries, and that alone makes it tastier."

Jewel's stomach roared. "I gotta go."

"Hey," Beth said. "Is it true you'll be filming for months with that show? One guy from the crew came in this morning and said this is ongoing."

Jewel snorted. "In his dreams." She walked out and rushed back to the diner where two plates of spaghetti and meatballs sat waiting.

"You could've started."

"The boy has manners," Doc said before putting his paper down and shuffling toward the door.

"Thank you for waiting." She took her seat and twirled the first bit around the fork.

"You're welcome. How was the place? Are you snowed in?"

She chewed and swallowed and hummed because it was so good. "No, it was a mild disaster. I think I'm losing my mind." She held up her hand. "I might be okay, but the crew is losing their mind. They think we'll be filming for months."

Mason choked on his pasta but seemed to get it under control.

"Maybe once things fall into a routine, you'll want to do more."

She laughed so hard that she drew the attention of several nearby diners. "I'd rather poke my eye out with a screwdriver than spend any more time than I have to with them. This little project, and it is little, has one purpose."

"That is?" He cut a meatball in half and ate it.

"To right the wrongs. If in the process you get the house sold and your inheritance, then that's a bonus."

"You wouldn't extend the contract under any conditions?"

She considered his question and knew this was a one-and-done deal. "Not even for a million bucks."

"What about thirty-five million?"

She cocked her head to the side in confusion. "What's this all about?"

He took a last bite before pushing his plate aside.

"Did you read the contract?"

He'd asked that several times before, and it was getting old. "Why are you so obsessed about the contract?"

Mason rubbed his face. "Because you should've read the fine print. I asked you to read the contract. Dammit, Jewel. Why didn't you read it?"

# CHAPTER TWENTY-TWO

The spaghetti rolled in her stomach, and the acid in the sauce burned her throat.

"Hey, kids. Everything all right?" Maisey asked, sweeping the plates into one hand. "You want pie?"

Jewel couldn't speak.

"We're good, Maisey." Mason handed her two twenties and told her to keep the change.

"I love a good tipper. It shows the type of man he is. Appreciates the value of others and that he's not cheap." She nodded toward Mason. "This one's a keeper."

She heard Maisey, but her brain was screaming louder. "I just got screwed, right?" She turned to Maisey. "Sorry, Maise, I'm in a crisis."

"Sounds like you need cherry pie. I'll get one to go."

"No, I'm good."

Maisey laughed. "Honey, I've seen good, and you ain't it." She walked away, leaving her gardenia perfume hanging in the air.

"Who screwed me over? Sylvia? Matt?" She stared at him, but he couldn't look her in the eye. "Your father." She slammed her hands down, making the remaining silverware jump from the table. "I told you he was up to no good. He started all of this."

Mason hung his head. "It might have started with my father, but he's not the one that screwed you." He looked up, and all the color seemed to drain from his face. "I did."

If a heart could crush, then hers flattened under the weight of those words. "You used me?"

He looked around the diner. "Can we go someplace private and talk?"

"No!" She wasn't one to make a scene, but if this man wanted to use her in the most public sense, then she didn't care about how the town of Aspen Cove viewed him. "You manipulated me." She didn't even know what the contract said, but she could guess as she added up the pieces. "How long am I in an emotional prison?"

He reached for her hand. "Jewel, it's not like that."

"No?" She rose from her seat and stomped toward the door.

"Don't forget your pie." Maisey rushed over with not a single piece but an entire cherry pie boxed and ready to go. "I added a fork inside in case you couldn't wait. You can bring it back. You okay, sweetie?"

"Yep." She tucked the pie under her arm and walked out of the diner.

She wasn't okay; she was ready to murder someone, but she didn't know who the first victim would be. Part of her wanted to start with Mason's father because he was the catalyst. Next would be Matt and Sylvia, and last was Mason. She wasn't sure why she put him at the end of the list. It was most likely because his betrayal hurt the most, and he needed a slow, painful death. She was halfway in love with him. It was pure love—the kind that didn't depend on hormones for its fuel. Sure, there was an attraction there, and she certainly wanted him, but they hadn't sealed the deal.

"Oh my God, that's why he went to bed early." Was he protecting her? She couldn't think of another reason. Maybe he was protecting himself. The house of cards he built was tumbling, and he knew she'd find out. She was also a pro with power tools, and that had to put fear into him. Mason had seen her fifty ways to kill Matt list.

"Wait up, Jewel," Mason called from behind her.

She spun around to face him. "You leave me alone." Instead of walking to her store, she turned into the pharmacy, hoping he wouldn't follow her in there.

Agatha was at the counter.

"What can I do for you, honey?"

"I need to see the doctor." She clutched at her chest because it ached so badly. "I think I'm having a heart attack."

Agatha screamed, "Paul, 911, honey, swallow your chicken and get down here." She rushed Jewel and her pie to the exam room, where Sage stood near a counter, looking like she was taking inventory.

"What have we got?" She put down a roll of bandages and helped Jewel onto the table. Within seconds, the pie was out of her hand, and they strapped her to several monitors. Sage and Doc moved around her like they'd been working a lifetime together.

"Tell me what happened?" Doc asked. His normally gruff voice seemed softer.

"I was having lunch, and then my world exploded."

Doc frowned. "Describe the pain. It was an explosion?"

"What? No, I'm not in any pain. I mean, I am. My heart hurts."

"Trying to sort this out, kiddo." He looked at the

paper spitting out from the machine hooked to her chest by wires and patches. "Was it a sharp pain, or did it radiate for a while and spread out? Was there pain in your back? Left arm? Anything go numb?"

"He broke my heart."

Doc dropped the paper. "Are you telling me you interrupted my fried chicken because of man troubles?"

His chastising tone was back, and Jewel couldn't take it. Her eyes flooded, and the sobs spilled from her lips.

"I didn't read the contract."

Sage tucked a few things back in the cupboard. "I've got a baby to feed. It looks like you've got this under control."

Doc bristled. "Don't leave me here with a hysterical woman. Love problems aren't my specialty." He looked at the door. "Agatha, you're up."

Sage poked her head out the door. "Looks like she's on break. It's all you, Doc."

"Sage Bishop, if you leave me here alone, you're fired."

Jewel watched the two go back and forth.

"Good, because it's hard being a working mother. I could use the break." Sage brushed past him. "I'll see you tomorrow, Doc."

He let out a growl that would've sent a dog scurrying, but it only made her cry harder. His hand came to her back with a pat, and a tissue appeared in front of her face.

"Get yourself together, and we'll have a chat."

"Jewel?" Mason's voice came from the hallway.

"Go away," she called. "Doc, make him go away, or you'll have a patient, and it won't be me."

"You young ones are so volatile these days. What happened to courting a girl?" He walked out the door, but she could hear him. "Young man, I suggest you carry yourself out of here. If you need an appointment, Agatha will be back in thirty minutes."

Doc returned. "I take it this heartache has something to do with that boy."

Boy was an oversell. Mason was well into his thirties, but then again, he was still under his father's thumb, so maybe boy was an accurate description.

"He duped me."

Doc pulled up a chair and sat in front of the exam table. "Tell me the whole story." He crossed his arms and leaned back.

Jewel told him everything except the part of her trying to get Mason to move to the next step in the relationship. She wasn't going to paint herself in a bad light. People had been doing that enough for her recently.

"Do you love this boy?"

"He's hardly a boy."

"Young lady, I'm older than dirt, so everyone

under the age of sixty is a kid, and that young man will always be a boy to me."

He had a point. If a person was half her age, they seemed like a kid. In reality, they were, but she got his meaning.

"I could've loved him."

That made her eyes tear up more, and Doc let out a frustrated sigh. "Wipe your leaky lakes dry. I can't talk to you if you're blubbering about."

"Has anyone ever told you your bedside manner needs some work?"

He chuckled. "They wouldn't dare." He played with his bushy mustache, rolling the end until it looked like a handlebar of a bike.

"I've got many years under my belt, and I know a little about love." He leaned forward and rested his elbows on his knees. "Love ain't perfect, but when you find a person who makes your ticker speed up, it might be worth fighting for. Take my Agatha, for instance. She was a pain in my keister. That damn woman was like a sticky booger I couldn't get rid of. I did everything to dissuade her but dammit if she didn't think she knew better."

Jewel breathed in a shaky breath. "Did she?"

Doc grumbled. "It pains me to say it, but yes. She's good for me."

"But did she manipulate you?"

"Listen here, that woman does it day in and day

out. Do you think I want to eat kale? I know it's good for me, but have you had the stuff?"

"This isn't about kale."

"It never is Jewel. It's about another person seeing opportunities you don't. Even if their motives aren't always pure, look at the overall picture."

"When have Agatha's motives been less than pure?"

"Since the day she met me. It was square dancing. She hemmed her skirts on the short side and wore some frilly pantaloons that I couldn't help but notice. I'm old, but I'm not dead."

Despite the dire situation her life was in, she laughed. "We call them underwear or panties these days, Doc. I think pantaloons were back in the eighteen hundreds when you were a child."

"Now you're a comedian?" He questioned. "Sometimes when things look like something you don't want, maybe you have to look at them again through a different lens." He moved his neck left and right, and a sharp popping sound filled the air. "Creaky bones. Anyway, I don't know much about that young man. I've heard plenty, but what I've seen doesn't match the story everyone paints about him."

"Oh, he's everything people say. He's slimy and underhanded, and he'll sell your mama a car without tires."

"Maybe a house without a roof, but you probably got a good deal on it, regardless."

"I got a good deal."

Doc smiled. "See, he was fair to you."

She blew her nose and shook her head. "No, that's the point. He used me to sell his house."

"Darling, you knew that was the deal going in."

He was right. "I should've read the contract."

"What does it say?"

She swallowed the lump in her throat. "I don't know. I haven't read it."

"You're telling me you're in here blubbering about a broken heart, and you don't even know the details."

"I know they're bad. I know they have suckered me into something I didn't want to do."

He made a clucking noise while he shook his head. "You always double-check. You'd think you would've learned after that last mishap with the wall."

"You knew who I was too?"

"I'm old, but I'm not blind." He rubbed his eyes. "I've got 20/400 vision."

"You're a regular eagle eye there, Doc."

He stood and helped her down from the table. "Go read that contract and then decide if you want to take a hammer to his head. Just give me a little notice, so I have the sutures and bandages ready."

"What do I owe you?"

Doc followed her to the front of the store. "I could use tile work in the apartment."

"Deal." She picked up her pie sitting in plain view on the counter and walked out feeling better even though nothing was resolved.

When she got to her store, she found Beth stocking the snack aisle.

"Hey, boss, I got that delivery of Raspberry Zingers."

"They are all yours, girl."

"Nah, I'm over them, but have you tasted the Hostess Lemon Pies?"

"Nope, but enjoy." She breezed up the stairs and went straight to the drawer where she'd placed the contract.

She opened the refrigerator and pulled out a soda. She'd much rather have a beer, but she had to go back to work.

Sitting at the small kitchenette, she scoured the contract with a fine-tooth comb. When she finished, she just stared at her signature.

This was her fault because, once again, she'd taken someone's word. She was the captain of her ship, and it was going down, but not before she murdered the crew. She put the pie on the counter and dialed Doc.

"Get the sutures and bandages ready. Blood is about to spill."

"Not right now. I'm busy. It's time for *Days of our Lives, and* Lovey will murder me if I miss it. You'll have to schedule your murderous rage another time. Should I call and give the sheriff a heads-up?"

"No, I have a few things to take care of before I go to jail." When she hung up, she didn't feel as treacherous, but she was still pissed—mostly at herself. How could she let herself down again?

# CHAPTER TWENTY-THREE

Mason paced the living room of the reno house, waiting for Jewel to return.

"Where is she?" Sylvia asked. "She's wasting time, which means she's wasting money."

"Leave her alone. She deserves to take what time she needs to process what just happened." Mason didn't like Sylvia to begin with, but he liked her less with each passing minute.

"Did you know she purchased tile that cost this much?" She stomped her heel and pointed to the boxes of tile just delivered. "She's trying to sabotage the project, and we're only a day in."

"She isn't trying to sabotage anything." He felt the need to defend Jewel. She might be mad and never say another word to him, but he'd be damned if he let Sylvia and Matt steamroll over her. "She said the tile would look good on film. If you want to save your show, then I suggest you let the real talent take over and run it."

Matt took the hammer he held and threw it, hitting the wall and leaving a dent.

"I suggest you fix that," Jewel said as she walked in like she owned the place. "Mason, move the tile to the bathroom." She turned to Sylvia. "I read the contract, and I'm not doing six houses."

Mason waited for her to rail at him, but she moved past him into the bathroom. She had the demeanor of a drill sergeant telling the crew to get their stuff and get filming.

As soon as the camera went live, Jewel smiled.

"Welcome to a new episode of *Reno or Wreck It*. Today we're renovating a bathroom. It's kind of like renovating a life. Sometimes you have to tear everything down and toss it out before you can begin again."

She smiled as if nothing had made her day sour.

"Hey, honey," Matt said as he walked in. He didn't look fazed either. "What can I do to help."

She pushed him backward. "Stay out of my way, *sweetheart*, or I'll trample you." She let out a little giggle that only the people who truly knew her would know was fake. She picked up one tile. "Today, we're talking about building something from the ground up." She tapped her foot on the subfloor. "Anything built on a shaky foundation doesn't last." She looked past the cameraman to where Mason stood. He got the message loud and clear. "Never settle for less than what you want." She held up the tile. "This is Carrera marble, it's expensive, but it's quality and will last a lifetime. Anything destined for long-term should be something you can live with forever, which is why I always suggest going neutral."

He listened to her and realized she was telling two stories at once. Sure, she was talking about the renovation, but she chose her words carefully so those around her would know the message was for them as well.

For the next few hours, she secured the backer board and mixed the thin set. She talked to the camera as she placed the tile in the tub surround.

"It's important to pay attention to the details." She stopped and looked straight at the camera. "I seem to repeat the same mistakes. Does that happen to you?"

She placed the last tile. "Like I said, it's all in the details." She pointed to the tile surround and then the bench. "This was going to be a tub and shower combo, but there wasn't enough room for a big soaking tub, so Mason, the real estate agent, and I came up with this shower. It's luxe with its built-in bench and rain shower combo. Next week, we'll work on the second bathroom. Until tomorrow." She smiled and walked off the set.

"Jewel," Mason called after her. "We need to talk."

She marched next door, into her house, and gathered her clothes.

"Jewel, please talk to me."

She held up her hand. "Mason, if you want to live, I suggest you back away from me. I'm so mad at you I can spit fire." She waved her arms around, dropping the clothes she held to the floor. "What was all this about? Was it part of the plan? I thought you liked me."

He rushed toward her and pulled her into his arms. "I do. I more than like you."

She struggled to get free, but he held her tightly until she stopped fighting him. Her head rested against his chest.

"Why did you betray me? You talked me into doing the show. I thought it was because you cared about me, but it wasn't." She pushed away and got enough room between them to pound her fists on his chest.

He stood there and let her because he knew he deserved that and more. "Talking you into doing the show was for you. You were so bitter and angry."

"I have a right to be angry both then and now." She stepped back and bent over to pick up the clothes from the floor. "You used me to get what you wanted."

He couldn't deny it. It was never his intent, but it helped him. "That was never the plan. Yes, I talked you into doing the show because I thought that was what you wanted."

"One show. I wanted to do one renovation and be done with it."

"Then do the one show."

"I can't. Haven't you read the contract? If I don't complete everything, I'm in breach of contract, and I have to pay them back. Everything I have would go to them. Haven't I given them enough already?"

"I'll pay them. Just do the one renovation. What is it? Six episodes? I'll pay the fines and penalties out of my trust."

She shook her head. "This is all about your trust. You once told me not to let anyone tell you who you are."

"That's true. Don't let someone else define you."

"Well, the flip side of that coin is, if you listen to people, you might learn something about yourself. What I learned is my name should be Jade because that's how I'll walk through life from this point forward. Even you told me that weeks ago. It's all in the details, isn't it? Sometimes, what you see is what you get. Everyone in town thought you were slimy and underhanded, but I didn't. Maybe I was looking at you through rose-colored glasses. It turns out I wasn't paying attention to the details." She moved around like a cyclone, picking her things up as she went.

"What are you doing?"

"I'm getting my clothes and moving back to my hovel."

He let out a breath of exasperation. "This is your house, Jewel. I'll pack up and leave if that's what you want."

She stopped and dropped her clothes. "You're right. It is my house." She bent over and grabbed them again. "But I made a deal, and unlike some people, there is no fine print. What I say is what I mean. I agreed to refurb your house, and I said you could stay here until we finished it."

She was making him dizzy with all the swirling and twirling and dropping and retrieving, and her words sliced like a razor into his soul.

"Jewel," he pointed to her and then him. "This thing between us was real."

She stood tall and pulled back her shoulders. "There is nothing between us."

"You're wrong. You're not paying attention to the details now."

"No, *you're* wrong. I got the message loud and clear last night when you left me to go to sleep early. Why lead me on if you couldn't close the contract?"

He moved like a bolt of lightning toward her. "I

refused to screw up what we had by making love to you. And it would've been love because that's what I feel for you. How would you have felt if we'd made love last night and you found out about the contract today?"

She tried to back away, but he held her shoulders. "Why didn't you tell me?"

He groaned. "Geez, Jewel, I tried. You didn't want to talk about work. You wanted an evening free of stress. I tried so many times. Even that day in the diner, I asked you several times to read the contract, and you told me it was standard."

"You could've said it's a trick." She hugged her clothes tightly to her chest.

"But I didn't."

"That's the question you should ask yourself. If you loved me, why didn't you?"

"Because I was an idiot. I thought we could have the best of both worlds, but I was wrong. The only world I want to exist in is yours." He pulled her toward him and pressed his lips to hers. She fought him for a second and then melted against him. Her lips opened, and she let his tongue sweep over hers. He felt every bit of hurt in that kiss. She tasted of sadness and devastation, but he promised to turn that into happiness and joy. When he broke the kiss, he looked at her. "Don't leave. Stay here with me. I promise I'll make it right."

She stepped back. "You can't. You'd have to give up too much to be with me, and you'd never do that. Besides, it's a long way back into my heart from where you stand. I don't think you have it in you to try."

"You're wrong."

She shrugged. "About a lot of things, but you?" She shook her head. "I should've listened to what people were saying."

She pushed past him and walked out the door.

Mason stared at where she once stood. The ache in his chest made him stagger. Was she gone from his life for good?

# CHAPTER TWENTY-FOUR

What a nightmare—literally. Jewel climbed out of bed and padded across the room to the kitchen sink. Her bare feet stuck to the still damp underflooring. If she weren't so exhausted, she would've laid down the new flooring she'd ordered for the flat.

She turned on the tap and poured herself a glass of water and flopped into a nearby chair. Faking happiness drained her. It had been a week since the fallout, and while she showed up to the site daily, her mind tried to be somewhere else because being present was too heartbreaking.

Working with Matt just pissed her off. Having to play nice with him made her want to take a shower in lye each night.

Working with Sylvia made her feel hollow. What woman sought her best friend's husband and underhandedly ruined a marriage? She shook her head. That was wrong because you can't break up a good marriage. The only way for it to erode is to have tiny fissures in it already.

Working with Mason eviscerated her. She didn't know why it hurt so badly, but it did. Maybe it was because he was the first man she trusted since the big betrayal.

The only thing about the project that felt good was the work. The master bath turned out beautifully with the black-and-white marble and black cabinetry. The hall bath wasn't much of a challenge either. She gutted and refurbished it with a new tub, the same marble flooring and cabinets, and a dove gray paint. They only had a few more days of filming for this house, and she'd be done—with this house, anyway.

Each time she thought about how Mason hoodwinked her into signing the contract, she wanted to get her nail gun out and put it to work.

She didn't have anyone to blame but herself. He had told her several times to look at the contract. What she couldn't understand was why he didn't come right out and tell her if she signed it, she would be stuck doing six other houses.

She gulped down the water and headed back toward the bed on the other side of her apartment. She would rather call it a flat because that sounded better than a flophouse.

Knowing she wouldn't get back to sleep, she dressed and started on the floor. It was a less expensive modular flooring that clicked into place, so she didn't need power tools.

She glanced at the color and wondered why everything she picked was some kind of gray lately and chalked it up to her mood.

She shifted the bed out of place and started in that corner. Sleeping on the double bed was part of the reason she couldn't sleep. The other was because she missed the warmth of Mason's body and the way he seemed to wrap around her in a protective coating.

"Some protection he offered." She shoved the flooring into place and clicked it down to lock. Before she knew it, she was halfway done and already physically worn out.

She stopped there and made a pot of coffee when her phone alarm rang. There were only a few days left until the open house, which they staged for this property. The town's residents were offered fifty dollars if they'd come and take a walk around pretending to be buyers. What she didn't tell Sylvia was that they would've done it for free. But watching her former bestie peel fifty-dollar bills from her budget gave Jewel a tiny thrill.

She poured her coffee into a to-go mug and took the stairs down into the grocery store. It was a nice perk to own a massive pantry and refrigerator. It made meals less boring. Today she grabbed a Honeybun and left.

With the sun just rising over Mount Meeker, the sky's hue was pink. It hadn't snowed since the time she left the windows open in her hovel, and with the warmer weather, things were sprouting, like the tiniest part of the daylilies peeking through the cold ground. Here and there, a confused crocus poked through as well.

Jewel knew it was a false hope that the dark, dreary cold was behind them. In the Rockies, it could snow into June or July.

She pulled into her driveway, right behind Mason's Mercedes. To look at both of their luxury cars was a laugh—a Porsche and a Mercedes in the driveway of a starter home neighborhood.

As she got out, her nose lifted into the air, and she caught a whiff of bacon. He was a Julia Child in Levi's and steel-toed boots. She missed his waffles and pancakes and cheese blintzes. He always made her coffee special with a dash of cinnamon. When she tried to make it, it tasted like cinnamon floating on her coffee, but when he made it, it tasted like heaven.

The door opened, and he poked his head out.

"Hey, I made you breakfast."

Her body leaned toward her house, but her brain tugged her toward the renovation.

"Thanks, but no thanks."

He let out a groan. "Come on, Jewel, can't we talk?"

"I've got nothing to say."

"Okay, then come in and eat in silence." She took a step forward, not sure what to do. A part of her wanted to mend the fences with Mason. She understood why he worked on her to accept the initial job. She even got why he signed on for the other six. Everyone wanted to make their parents proud, or at least make them think you've done a good job. Selling the two houses for Elite was expected. It was part of the terms to get his trust fund. The other six were the icing on the cake—not required—just a bonus.

Given that Aspen Cove was a tiny blink of a town, it wasn't as if everyone and their brother were rushing to move there. It could take Mason years to sell those properties. Brokering a deal with Sylvia was a savvy business decision. Too bad it screwed her in the process.

"I'm still mad at you."

"I know, and that's okay, but I made you eggs Benedict, and you said you'd do anything for eggs Benedict. All I'm asking is for you to come in and eat. You don't have to say a word."

Her stomach grumbled, and she knew the Honeybun she scarfed down on the way there wouldn't hold her.

"Fine, but only because I'm hungry." She looked toward the reno house.

"You've got an hour before everyone shows up."

With a sigh, she walked into her house and the smell of happiness. Nothing made her feel better than eggs, Canadian bacon, English muffins, and a creamy, buttery sauce.

"Smells good." She took her usual seat at the table and waited.

Mason took a cinnamon stick and grated it into a cup before putting on a drizzle of honey and topping it with coffee. Maybe that was the key. He used quality ingredients.

"I miss your coffee."

He set the mug in front of her. "I'd make it every day for you. All you have to do is ask."

She took him in, dressed in faded jeans and a baby-blue T-shirt that hugged his chest like she did when she thought he was sleeping. He looked almost as good as the eggs he plated up. Even from this distance, she could see they were perfectly poached, and the hollandaise was thick and creamy.

When he set it on the table, a sense of euphoria washed over her. It was like the last couple of weeks disappeared, and they were back together. Not together, together, because they had never discussed that, but at least on the same page as each other.

"Taste it and let me know if I'm missing anything."

She cut a bite and mopped it through the sauce before trying it.

It was a tongue orgasm that rushed through her entire body, making her hum from the inside out.

"So good." She sipped her coffee and let her joy come out in a sigh. "Better than the junk I've been eating the last few days." She took another bite. "I'm proof that you can live on Red Vines and Pop-Tarts and survive."

He shook his head and made a clicking sound with his tongue. "You know that's not healthy."

"Yeah, I know, but I made a new list."

His brows lifted. "*Fifty ways to kill yourself?*"

"No, I made that last week."

His shoulders dropped, and she regretted saying that. No matter what Mason had done and whatever his motives were at the time, he was a decent human being.

"No, 50 *Things I can eat for breakfast.*" She

dragged another bite through the sauce and popped it into her mouth. When she swallowed, she said, "You can also live off of sunflower seeds, cheese sticks, and baby carrots for breakfast."

He sat across from her with his plate. "I'm sorry."

She liked that he kept telling her that, but sorry didn't make it better.

"I can't say it's okay because it's not. I have life plans too, and working for the next year on those houses wasn't part of them. I don't want to have to deal with my ex on the daily. All I want to do is fix my house and run the store."

"You hate that store."

She shifted in her seat. "I don't hate it; it's just not where I thought I'd be. I feel like my life has taken a detour. It was like I was on my way to see the Grand Canyon, and somehow I ended up in Lake Tahoe. Both are beautiful, but they're different. It's an adjustment."

He swallowed his bite and smiled. That smile made her insides melt.

"I get it. I was on my way to my penthouse and wound up in renovation. It was far from where I thought I'd be, but I've learned a lot along the way." He stood up and grabbed a notepad that sat on the counter. "I made a list of things too."

He opened the cover and turned the page toward her.

On the top of the sheet was the title, *Fifty ways to live a better life.* Below it was a bulleted list.

- Be honest
- Be a good human
- Listen more than you speak
- Eat your vegetables
- Love deeply
- Love Jewel
- Make it up to Jewel
- Make love to Jewel
- Tell Jewel you're sorry until she forgives you
- Make Jewel your priority
- Define what's valuable in your life ... Jewel
- Let go of unimportant things
- Be prepared to sacrifice

The list went on and on and ended with

- Tell her you love her

She rubbed her finger over the last entry, and a tear fell from her eye and splashed on the page, making the ink run on the word love.

She pushed her chair back so hard it hit the wall. "I can't do this." She moved to the door.

He caught her before she could escape.

"Don't run. I swear I'll make this right. I love you. Until you, I didn't know what I should value in my life. Nothing matters if you don't have someone to share it with."

She struggled to free herself, but his arms wrapped around her like a vise.

"Please let me go," she cried. "I can't do this." She pushed against his chest until he released her and stepped back. She ran out the front door and straight to her car.

She was back in her place, curled in a ball on her bed five minutes later.

That's where she stayed for three days. She only left to go downstairs after hours and picked up the overage of Raspberry Zingers. They were the sweetest part of Mason.

She hated lying to herself. It was his kisses and hugs and now his eggs Benedict.

Her phone rang again, and Sylvia's face showed on her screen. She knew she needed to answer it, or she'd be in big legal trouble.

"I'll be in tomorrow," she said.

"Good, because the lawyers are ready to move forward with a breach of contract suit."

"I said I'd be in tomorrow, but I'm not doing the other houses." She'd decided over the last few days that working with Matt and Sylvia was like being repeatedly tortured. It was emotional waterboarding of sorts.

"If you walk away, I'll take everything."

She didn't have the energy to care. "You can have it. You took everything I had once before, and I survived." She hung up, feeling free for the first time in weeks.

# CHAPTER TWENTY-FIVE

Mason left Aspen Cove the second day Jewel was absent. If she didn't show up soon, the contract would be void. The funny thing was, he didn't care.

He'd lose it all, including his trust fund, but the only thing that made him ache inside was losing her.

He'd rather live in squalor than live without Jewel.

He adjusted his tie and walked into Elite Properties. It was an enormous glass building in downtown Denver. His father built it on the premise that a glass building gave people the idea you were transparent, but that was all a facade. There was nothing transparent about Trenton Van der Veen—he was all smoke and mirrors.

"Hello, Mason," his dad's secretary said when he entered the top floor office.

"Good morning, Madge. You look beautiful today." She wasn't a day younger than seventy, and her white hair always coifed perfectly into what his mother once called a chignon. She had the face of a forty-year-old. If he hadn't attended her fortieth birthday when he was a child, he would've sworn she was an anti-aging sorceress.

"You're a charmer just like your father." She blushed and tilted her head coyly down. "He's waiting for you." She rose from her chair and smoothed out her skirt. "Would you like a coffee?"

He shook his head. "No, I don't plan on staying long."

She tittered in a high pitch. "Plans are one thing. Reality is another. You still like it with cinnamon and honey?"

"Yes, that would be lovely." He always tried to treat people with kindness and respect. He was blunt and to the point, but he never wanted to be deceitful, which made the whole situation with Jewel worse. But he figured she would've read the contract and seen that six houses were in there. After her lack of attention to detail, he was sure she'd never take anyone's word for a thing again. He should've just told her, but he didn't. Losing her scared him, and that's what happened, anyway.

He opened the door and walked into his father's office.

"Mason," the gruff voice said while pointing to the seat in front of the desk. While his father's chair was fit for a king, these were the chairs meant for the serfs. They sat low to the ground and forced you to look up. Everything about his father's life put him in a position of power, from the size of his desk to the red tie he always wore.

"Thanks for meeting with me." He sat and felt like a teen staring up at his father. In his pocket was his resignation letter. Though he'd already been let go, he knew how his father was, and after the renovation and sale of the house, he'd be back at work.

The last few days, he looked at what his life would be like and feel like. He wasn't ready to slide back into place—his place as his father's whipping post.

He pulled the letter from his pocket and passed it across the dark mahogany desk. It was funny how everything surrounding them was hard and cold, from the solid wood furnishings to the stone floors and glass.

The only warmth Mason had ever known came from his mostly absent mother and Heidi, who loved him like the child she never had. In her eyes, he could do no wrong. In his father's eyes, all he did was disappoint.

"What's this?"

"It's my resignation letter."

A rolling laugh moved through his father and came out in decibels high enough to cause hearing loss.

"I already let you go, boy."

"I know." The door opened and in walked Madge with his coffee. She disappeared just as quickly as she arrived. She'd worked here long enough to recognize the unfriendly look on his father's face.

Mason held the cup in his palms and let the heat warm his icy hands. "This is an all-encompassing resignation. I know how you work, and if I told you I'd brokered a deal to have the other six homes featured on *Reno or Wreck It*, you'd bring me back on just to manage it."

"Did you?" Trenton leaned forward.

"I did."

His father gave him a single clap, then rubbed his hands together like he was plotting to take over the world.

"That means they'll pay for the renovations, right?"

"And guarantee a sale."

Knowing his father was excited filled him with a sense of pride. He had done all of that, but it was for naught.

"My boy, I knew you had it in you."

He was so close to falling for the false high that his father's admiration gave. He pulled the coffee cup to his lips and took a sip, and reality slid back in.

Mason cleared his throat and hoped he could get through the rest of the news he had to deliver. "When you sent the news crew to give Jewel a hard time and to sabotage me, you let the world know where she was, which brought the show back into her life."

"I like that one. She has some talent."

Mason took another drink of his coffee. "I like her too. So much so that I'm willing to sacrifice everything for her."

When his father's head cocked, his jowls shook. "What do you mean?"

He pointed to the letter. "I'm walking away from everything. You. The Trust. The houses in Aspen Cove. Everything. You sent me there as a punishment, and at first, I was in hell, but things changed because of Jewel."

"You're what?" His father bellowed.

Mason was certain his father's voice shook the windows. "I'm out."

"You don't get to quit this family. I brought you into this world and—"

"I know. You can take me out. I've got that line memorized. You know, Dad, you're completely out of touch with reality. You may rule your world, but not everyone lives in your world."

"You can walk away from me, but don't forget, my DNA runs through you. You'll always be a Van der Veen."

He nodded. "Yes, and it saddens me."

"Get out." His father pointed to the door.

"No problem, but before I go, I want to know who made you like this? Was it your father?" He hadn't spent much time with his grandparents. His father's father died early of a heart attack. "I can't imagine any man being proud of his son and driving them to make the sale no matter what. I'm ashamed of who I was, but I'm proud of who I've become."

"You're a disappointment."

That should've hurt, but it didn't. "You know what? I'd rather let you down than let myself down. When it comes to morals, you set the bar low. To raise my standards, I have to let it all go."

"Where will you be?"

He didn't know. He had some money put away, not enough to live comfortably forever on, but he wouldn't starve. "If you need me in the next couple of days, you can find me in Aspen Cove. After that," he shrugged. "I have no idea." His entire life had been planned out for him, but now it was time to figure it out for himself. "I imagine most fathers want their sons to grow up to be good men. Walking away from this is the first manly thing I've ever done. You should be proud."

His father's fists hit the top of the table with a bang. "Right now, I'm pissed."

"Well, that happens too. Heidi used to tell me I could get glad in the same shoes I got mad in." He chuckled. "No doubt some ugly Italian driving moccasins." He turned to the door. "No matter what, the house next to Jewel's is nearly done. You should come to look at it. She took it from slumlord to spectacular. The show should air soon."

"The show?"

"Yes, *Reno or Wreck It* showcased it and the remodel. You should be happy about that. You'll get lots of free airtime. Hope it was worth it."

He walked out the door and stopped at Madge's desk.

"Have a good day, Madge."

She stared at the closed door and then turned back to him. "Everything all right?"

He smiled. "It's almost perfect."

# CHAPTER TWENTY-SIX

Jewel came downstairs to find Beth with three candy bars and a box of Raspberry Zingers sitting on the counter in front of her. For a woman who consumed her weight in sugar daily, she was growing at an average pace. The tiny baby bump was slightly pronounced, but she certainly didn't look like she gorged on pastries and chocolate all day.

"Bad day?"

"Never let your mother move next door." She opened a Snickers and took a bite. "Not only is she driving me crazy, but she's driving the neighborhood nuts too. All she does is make cupcakes and hand-deliver them. I swear she's trying to wipe out the entire block with diabetes."

Jewel looked at the collection Beth gathered. "Family habit?"

She shook her head. "Oh no, this is medicinal. Besides, all she makes me is zucchini or bran muffins. But everyone else gets double chocolate fudge or white chocolate macadamia nut. Me, I'm stuck with carrot or some other vegetable muffin better suited for soup than sweets."

"You work across the street from one of the best bakeries in Colorado. You can sneak over there for your fix."

Beth spread her hands out like a game show host. "Why when I have the coolest boss in town who lets me order what I want and eat what I want."

"Will I make a profit this month, or are you eating my rent money?" The thought of rent money made her feel sick. She could pay her mortgage with the money she earned from the show. One episode paid her house payment for six months, but what if Sylvia came after her assets? It was one thing to say it didn't matter, but another to know that to be the truth.

"I've been upselling. I look to see what people are buying, and I suggest something to go with it. You know, like dessert when all they have is dinner fixings."

"Okay, carry on, but I'd watch the sugar intake because that's not good for you or the baby."

Beth's jaw dropped. "Have you been talking to my mother? I swear she's going to—"

Jewel held up her hand. "I don't even know your mom."

"Oh yes, you do. She's the one who looks like a librarian with a secret room for naughty boys."

"Oh, that's your mom." Jewel laughed. "Be glad you have your mom. I lost both of my parents in a plane crash, and I miss them every day."

"You're right." As if a light went on in Beth's head, she lit up. "I can loan you mine for a while."

She walked toward the door. "I could never replace my mom."

"What about Mason?"

The mention of his name made her insides flip. She told herself it was indigestion but knew it was that connection she and Mason had.

"What about him?"

"Can they replace him?"

"You have to have someone to replace them."

Beth waved her away. "Girl, you had that man like a fish on a hook." She took another nibble at the chocolate coating of her candy bar. "He came in this morning asking for boxes. I gave him what we had."

"Boxes? For what?"

"I guess he's moving, and he said he needed to pack up the last of his things."

Her heart stilled for a long second, then exploded

in her chest as if a bomb had detonated. "He's leaving?"

Jewel didn't wait for her response. She rushed out the front door and climbed into her SUV. When she arrived at the site, she saw his car parked in the driveway of her house. Along the curb was a moving truck.

She climbed out, slamming the door behind her, and marched inside the house to find it completely cleared out. Mason stood in the kitchen, handing the driver his credit card.

"Storage for now, but I'll let you know when I settle in somewhere." He turned and saw her standing in the doorway.

"You're leaving?" All the emotions roiling in her gut rose to her face. The heat on her cheeks was like a fire alarm fire. "You got what you wanted, and you're leaving me to carry the burden? What an asshole." She turned and walked away.

"Jewel, come back. That's not what's happening here."

She ignored his plea and stomped toward the renovation house. Only ten steps from the door and she saw Trenton Van der Veen.

"Can I speak to you?" he asked.

"No, you can't." She moved another two steps forward.

"I now own the production company, and therefore I believe I own you. I suggest you take a few minutes and talk to me."

His words were like a splash of ice water on her face.

"Oh, that's rich. You get your son to stir up a bunch of shit and me to renovate your house and sign my life away on another contract, and then he leaves, and you buy out the company. Was this the plan all along?"

She fisted her hips and dug them into her sides so that she didn't reach for a power tool. In her mind, there was a list building, one that had Mr. Van der Veen's name at the top.

"No, but it's brilliant. I don't like that my son walked away from everything." He rubbed his clean-shaven jaw. "But he had a genius moment that might serve Elite Properties. Who knew the boy had it in him."

She was still stuck on *he walked away from everything*. "What do you mean he walked away?" Was it like she thought? Because he finished his work here, and now he'd go back to Denver and assume his old life?

"He came in and handed me a letter—a resignation letter."

"But you already fired him." Her hands slid from her hips to her sides.

"I know, but this was different. He was resigning

from my life. He told me he imagined most fathers wanted their sons to grow up to be good men, and walking away from me was the first manly thing he'd ever done and I should be proud."

"Are you?"

He grimaced. "At first, I was pissed. No one walks away from me, but after a glass of scotch and a talk with his mother, I realized that standing up to me is the manliest thing any man has ever done."

"So why buy the production company?"

"Turns out I had thirty-five million dollars I needed to invest. Mason also pointed out that this show would give Elite Properties lots of airtime."

"He's not getting his trust fund?" It appalled her they had both walked through a gauntlet, and he came out empty-handed.

"He walked away from it. He said he didn't want it. You know what else he said?"

"I don't have a clue." And she didn't. She couldn't understand the power dynamics of his family because hers was so different. Her family worked construction, but they never worked against each other.

"He said he was in hell until he met you or something like that. I think my boy gave it all up for you."

"Not for me." She pointed toward the moving truck that was pulling away. "He's leaving."

"Only because you don't want him to stay."

"That's not true."

"Really? Have you told him you love him?"

She bristled. "I don't love him."

"Are you sure?"

Was she? "I'm in like with him."

"Woman, I've loved many women, and many women have loved me. I know what that emotion looks like, and you're in love with my son. While I wouldn't give a damn thing up for a woman, I admire that he's willing to step away from it all for something he believes in—you."

"Maybe it has nothing to do with me and everything to do with not wanting to be like you."

"He's never been like me. No matter how much I tried to mold him into me, he was always him, and in hindsight, I think that's a good thing. The world wouldn't know what to do with two of me."

"Excuse me," Sylvia asked. "The crew is ready for you." She smiled at Trenton in the same way she smiled at Matt when they first met.

"Leave it be, Sylvia. He's married."

Sylvia rolled her eyes. "That's never been a roadblock before."

"Not something I'd brag about, especially in front of your new boss."

"We're filming the wrap-up in five, don't be late, or your new boss won't be happy." She turned and walked back inside.

"A little advice." She thumbed over her shoulder. "That one is trouble. Oh, and since you are the new boss, you should know that after this house, I quit."

"I figured as much." He nodded toward the door. "You better get in there and say what you have to say. And Jewel ... don't forget that my son loves you. He's not like me. He's his own man, and that makes him better than me. When you're done, we'll talk about your contract."

"Right, the contract." Her stomach knotted. There was an actual chance she'd lose everything, but she didn't have as much to lose as Mason. "You should give him his trust fund. He earned it." She spun on her boots and walked inside.

The crew was there waiting for her with a script. She took it from Sylvia and read over the hollow words about her being so happy to be back.

She smiled and tucked it into her back pocket.

"Don't you need that?" Sylvia asked.

"I got it."

"Okay, then let's roll," the cameraman said.

She looked at the camera and smiled. "Hello, I'm your host, Jewel Monroe." She stalled for a moment, thinking maybe she should go with the script, but then she saw Mason walk in and something took over —her heart. "Ever walk into a house and think there's no hope for this one?" She chuckled and moved to the kitchen. "A house is like a person. The kitchen is the heart of the home, and this one was fractured when we showed up. I say we because this started as a personal project with Mason Van der Veen." She looked up at him and watched his head cock to the right. Though he'd been on set the whole time, no one had ever mentioned him.

"We worked well as a team. Mason was the team's heart and he said I was the talent, but that's not true. Anyway, I digress. The kitchen is the heart of the home, and this one was in cardiac arrest when we began, but as you can see, we put it on a steady diet of tender loving care, and it transformed. All this space needed was someone to see its potential." She stared at him again. "I see yours." She knew the at-home audience would think she spoke to them, but she was talking to Mason. She only hoped he knew the words were for him. He'd given up everything and probably because she told him he could never make it right because it would cost him too much. "The living area is the body, with the bedrooms and bathrooms being the limbs. Sometimes a house is so worn and weary that you think it's beyond repair. Have you ever taken the time to stand in the center and be silent and listen? Listen to the house speak to you? In our crazy world, we rarely embrace the silence and the messages that come to us in the quiet moments. So, the next time you see a house whose foundation is weak or built on shaky ground, and you think it's not worth salvaging, remember that tenderness, care, and love can fix everything." She moved toward Mason and stood in front of him. "I'm sorry, and I love you. You're the foundation that I want to build my life on. You're the heart in my kitchen, the hands to my limbs, and we'll figure out the rest later."

"I'm giving up my trust fund. I have nothing to offer."

She lifted on tiptoes. "Not true, you make a mean eggs Benedict."

He pulled her into his arms and whispered in her ear. "If my things weren't halfway to storage, I'd take you to my bed and show you how I feel about you."

She grabbed his hand and pulled him out of the house. "I've got you covered." She tossed him the keys to her Porsche. "Hurry." She reached into her bag and pulled out her pen and pad of paper.

"What are you doing?"

"Making a list, of course." She scribbled across the top and turned the page to show him.

*Fifty ways to show Mason I love him.*

"I don't need fifty, baby. All I need is to hear those three little words." He backed off the driveway and stopped to look at her.

She noticed the crew still filming her, so she rolled down the window and yelled, "That's a wrap."

Mason laughed. "That wasn't what I was going for, but it'll do."

"I love you," she said.

# CHAPTER TWENTY-SEVEN

They didn't leave her tiny apartment for two days and wouldn't have except his father called and wanted to discuss Jewel's contract. There was no way he'd let Jewel meet with his father alone.

She could handle herself, but he'd feel better if he could be the silent observer and clue her in as soon as he saw the telltale signs of his father's manipulation.

"You ready?" he asked.

She came out of the bathroom shrugging on a navy-blue blazer she paired with her jeans.

"You think he'll come after the apartment and the store? What about the house?"

Mason looked around the tiny space they'd been living in. "Commercial property isn't his thing."

"Why does he want to meet us at the house?"

"I told him he should look at it. Maybe he will."

They walked down the stairs into the store.

"Condoms are on aisle nine," Beth said. "She patted her stomach. Just don't let my mom near them."

"We haven't talked about kids," he said.

Jewel giggled. "We haven't done much talking at all. You've been few words and all action." Her body wiggled from her hair to her toes. "I love a man of action."

He tugged her toward the door. "You love me."

"True."

Once outside, they found her car, where they parked it two days ago, and drove to the house.

His father's Mercedes sat out front.

"Well, here goes nothing." Jewel squared her shoulders and exited the car.

She was an independent woman and never waited for him to open her door, but she never stopped him from cooking for her. Jewel's talents weren't culinary. Her skills lay in the bedroom and building. That woman could be the death of him, but she was the life in him too.

"Mason," his father said, looking past Jewel. His eyes dropped to her. "Jewel."

Over the two days they were gone, the house was staged and looked like a model home.

"Wow," Jewel inched past his father and into the house. "This is when you can see the difference. It's like when a girl puts on a dress and lipstick or, in my case, a blazer." She tugged at the lapels. "Fancies up the place."

"We've got an open house."

Mason's eyes went wide. "Who's the agent?"

His father tugged at his tie. "I am. I'm getting back to basics. It seems like I've been out of touch for a while. I've heard the whispers."

Mason chuckled. "Oh, I didn't whisper. I bellowed at you."

His father pointed to the table, which had a stack of papers sitting on it. "Shall we get started?"

"I'm not going to refurbish the houses for you. I refuse to work with my cheating ex and the promiscuous producer. I signed that contract thinking it was the standard, but there was fine print."

"There's always fine print," his father said. "The first rule in business is to read what's written between the lines."

He pushed a packet of papers in front of both of them.

"By the way, your mother and I are finally getting divorced. I expedited the process, and things should be completed by the end of the month."

Mason shook his head. "Why now? You've been living away from each other for years."

"A wise man showed me that hanging on to the past will hurt my chances at a happy future. Your mom is my past."

"And Sable is your future?"

He laughed. "No, she's just a good masseuse with talented hands, but I let her go too. I'm turning over a new leaf."

"Why?" Mason didn't understand the total turn-around. This man sitting in front of him wasn't his father.

"You asked the other day if I was happy, and the answer is no. Having you walk out of my life made me realize I focus too much on the wrong things. I need a Jewel in my life."

Mason wrapped his arm around her. "This one is mine."

"I can see that." He pointed to the packets. "Open to page one, and you'll see that I've turned over the six houses and the production company to you. Your trust paid for them, anyway. This allows you to approach the properties in any way you see fit. Jewel no longer works for me but works for you. If you want to let her go from her contract, that's your choice. You want to dissolve the show, that's fine too, although I can see the benefit for Elite Properties, and we'd be happy to entertain a partnership with you if you kept the show on the air. Of course, I imagine Jewel will be busy doing her own thing or possibly giving me a grandson, so maybe an occasional guest visit would be nice."

Mason stared at his father. "You're giving me this with no strings attached?"

His father raised his hands in surrender. "Not a one. You're a man who has proven he can make choices for himself. The minute you chose to go on your own is the exact second I knew I'd raised you right. You have a backbone, son, and that makes me proud."

How many years had he been waiting to hear those words? "I'm a little confused."

"I get it. I'm like a case of whiplash but better that than a case of hives."

A shadow fell upon them. "Hello, can I come in?"

His father jumped up, but before he dashed to the woman in the doorway, he said, "There's an envelope in the back. That's for you, son." He walked forward as Mason and Jewel sat watching. "I'm Trenton Van der Veen, and you are?"

"I'm Elsa Buchanan, and I'm hoping you're the answer to my dreams."

Mason saw a slight twinkle in his father's eyes. "Oh, I am. I surely am. Shall we start in the bedrooms?"

As soon as they walked out of sight, he turned the pages until he reached the envelope, and when he opened it and saw the transfer for twenty million dollars, he nearly fell off his seat. "He gave me my trust. It's all here in cash, assets, and a production company. I don't get it."

She leaned into him. "Read between the lines, Mason. He's telling you he loves you."

He shook his head. "After all these years."

"Sometimes, you have to lose something before you understand its value." He knew she was speaking about them.

"I'll never let you go," he said.

"I'll never leave." She turned to the front page. "Are you going to keep the production company?"

"I don't know. What do you think?"

She rubbed her chin. "Can I fire the producer and the beefcake?"

"Absolutely."

"Then I'd say, yes, let's see where we can take this. It's your company, your rules."

He shook his head. "Nope," he turned the packet several pages. While he'd been looking through the documents, he saw the blank paperwork. He didn't know why his father put it in there. One thing that would never change about Trenton Van der Veen was his need to manipulate, but in this case, it worked out in his favor. "I'm turning over the company as an engagement present."

"Are you asking me to marry you?"

"Not today, but it's a promise that someday soon I will."

She smiled. "You know, most people ask with a ring."

"I'm not like most people. I'm a Van der Veen."

She laughed. "I've been warned."

Voices came from the hallway. "So, it's a deal?" His father asked.

"We can discuss it over dinner at Trevi's Steakhouse. You can pick me up at six and don't wear that red tie. Tonight, I'm in charge."

Mason nearly choked as his father escorted the woman outside.

"What the hell was that?"

Jewel giggled. "According to Beth, that's trouble."

"God help us."

"No, God help your father because I'm fairly certain he's just met his match."

Next up is One Hundred Reflections

# OTHER BOOKS BY KELLY COLLINS

**An Aspen Cove Romance Series**

*One Hundred Reasons*

*One Hundred Heartbeats*

*One Hundred Wishes*

*One Hundred Promises*

*One Hundred Excuses*

*One Hundred Christmas Kisses*

*One Hundred Lifetimes*

*One Hundred Ways*

*One Hundred Goodbyes*

*One Hundred Secrets*

*One Hundred Regrets*

*One Hundred Choices*

*One Hundred Decisions*

*One Hundred Glances*

*One Hundred Lessons*

*One Hundred Mistakes*

*One Hundred Nights*

*One Hundred Whispers*
*One Hundred Reflections*
*One Hundred Chances*
*One Hundred Dreams*

# GET A FREE BOOK.

Go to www.authorkellycollins.com

# ABOUT THE AUTHOR

International bestselling author of more than thirty novels, Kelly Collins writes with the intention of keeping love alive. Always a romantic, she blends real-life events with her vivid imagination to create characters and stories that lovers of contemporary romance, new adult, and romantic suspense will return to again and again.

*For More Information*
www.authorkellycollins.com
kelly@authorkellycollins.com

Made in the USA
Monee, IL
05 August 2023

40495909R00157